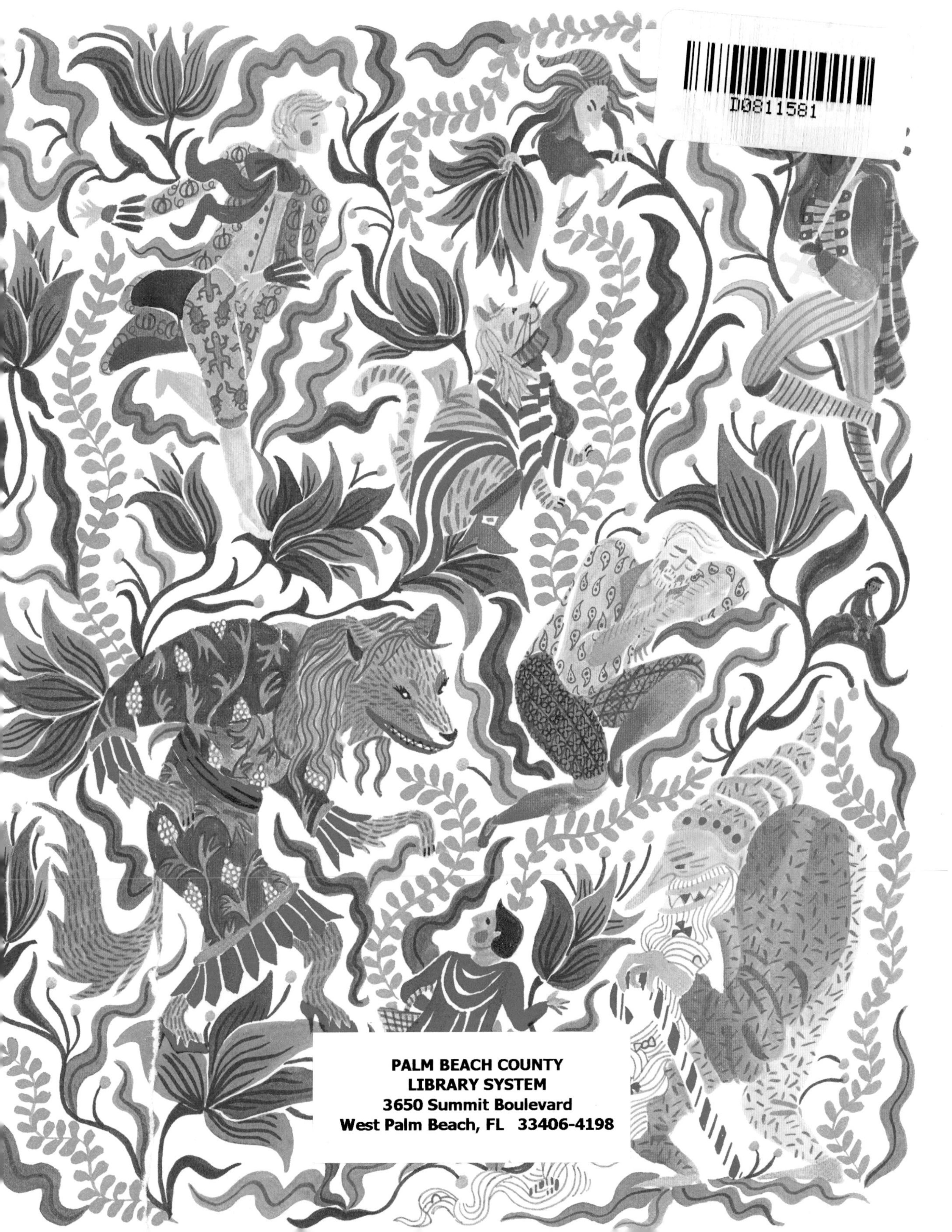

GENDER SWAPPED
FAIRY TALES

KARRIE FRANSMAN & JONATHAN PLACKETT

GENDER
SWAPPED

FAIRY TALES

faber

First published in 2020
by Faber & Faber Limited
Bloomsbury House
74–77 Great Russell Street
London WC1B 3DA

Typeset by Faber & Faber Limited
Printed and bound in Slovenia by DZS-Grafik d.o.o.

A CIP record for this book
is available from the British Library

ISBN 978–0–571–36018–5

6 8 10 9 7 5

For Lyra
(the other thing we made together)

CONTENTS

Authors' Note

xiii

Handsome and the Beast

3

Cinder, or the Little Glass Slipper

35

How to Tell a True Prince

47

Jacqueline and the Beanstalk

51

Gretel and Hansel

71

Mr Rapunzel

85

Snowdrop

95

Little Red Riding Hood

111

The Sleeping Handsome in the Wood

119

Frau Rumpelstiltzkin

137

Mistress Puss in Boots

145

Thumbelin

157

Acknowledgements

173

Snowdrop

95

Little Red Riding Hood

111

The Sleeping Handsome in the Wood

119

Frau Rumpelstiltzkin

137

Mistress Puss in Boots

145

Thumbelin

157

Acknowledgements

173

AUTHORS' NOTE

Dear Reader,

Thank you for taking the time to read *Gender Swapped Fairy Tales*. We would love to begin with the story behind our book.

Jonathan Plackett: When I was a little boy, my father would read me and my sister bedtime stories. Unbeknown to us, he would secretly swap the genders of the characters in the books. This made the stories far more interesting for him to read, and provided us with exciting, fresh characters who didn't conform to old gender stereotypes.

Fast forward thirty years and I'm now a creative technologist and married to comic writer and artist Karrie Fransman. We have a daughter of our own, who we want to grow up in a world where little girls can be powerful and where little boys can express their vulnerability without anger.

I wondered if it would be possible to create a computer algorithm that swapped all gendered language in any text, turning 'he' to 'she', 'Mrs' to 'Mr' and 'daughters' to 'sons'. After some surprising and protracted battles with the oddities of the English language, I managed to create an easy-to-use computer program that could swap the gender of any text you threw at it.

Karrie Fransman: I was fascinated when Jonathan showed me the algorithm and we wondered how we could use it in the real world. I suggested applying it to gender-swap fairy tales. We loved the idea of mixing classic texts with modern technology, updating these stories for a contemporary reader. As a comic creator I was also excited to see how the algorithm would transform some of the world's best tales and then imagine those new stories in illustration.

We chose to use the public-domain, infamous Fairy Books, edited by Andrew Lang and published between 1889 and 1913. This gorgeous, multicoloured series collected the very best tales from all over the world and popularised them for a mass audience, including stories by Gabrielle-Suzanne de Villeneuve ('Beauty and the Beast') and those collected by the Brothers Grimm ('Hansel and Gretel', 'Rumpelstiltskin', 'Snowdrop' and 'Rapunzel'). Rather serendipitously, these books were also edited by a wife-and-husband team. It was Andrew Lang who rose to fame, with his name appearing on the covers as editor. However, researcher Andrea Day has suggested (in '"Almost wholly the work of Mrs Lang": Nora Lang, Literary Labour, and the Fairy

Books', in *Women's Writing*, 2017) that in fact it was his wife, Leonora Blanche 'Nora' Lang, who did most of the work, particularly in the later books in the series. We found this to be a very happy coincidence, given what we intended to do to the original texts!

Fairy tales are the ideal genre to gender swap. They are some of the earliest stories we are exposed to as children and form the very building blocks of storytelling. They allow us to live out fantasies, inhabit roles and defeat monsters. Most importantly they teach us the difference between 'good' and 'evil' and about the moral codes that govern our society: that boys should bravely scale giant beanstalks to claim what is rightfully theirs, or that little girls should be wary of talking to strangers in dark woods. However, these tales also contain all the magic and possibility of fairy dust. If we can imagine a world where harps sing and rats transform into coachmen, can we not (with a little help from a gender-swapping algorithm) also imagine a world where kings want kids and where old women aren't witches?

With that, *Gender Swapped Fairy Tales* was born. It's important here to stop and talk about the word 'gender' and what we are 'swapping'. We should state that we are not suggesting that there are only two genders to swap. For the purposes of this discussion, we view the term 'sex' as focussing on the body and 'gender' as socially constructed. Most cultures divide gender into 'feminine' and 'masculine' and all the social roles, norms and behaviours that separate them. However, these days people are increasingly becoming comfortable inhabiting the space in between these dichotomised ideas of 'femininity' or 'masculinity'. We have people who identify as gender non-binary, queer, transgender, gender fluid, agender or other-gender and more. But the division of 'feminine' and 'masculine' is still prominent in most people's minds and also in language. By swapping these two dominant gender constructs, we want to disrupt this binary and ask people to question what assumptions we make about gender in society.

Jonathan: After running a few fairy tales through the gender-swapping algorithm, we knew that we were onto something special. Right before our eyes, fascinating new characters were created and stereotypes were laid bare. We saw princesses in shining armour racing to rescue their sleeping princes. Kings sat by windows sewing and longing for a child. Kind-hearted young men were rewarded for looking past the flaws of beastly princesses. The stories took on a new dimension, effortlessly highlighting the gender biases within the original text.

One of my initial motivations in creating the algorithm was to see the world from a perspective different to my own. While some of the changes were predictable, others revealed subtleties I hadn't noticed before, like how women now automatically came first, with 'sisters and brothers', and in titles like 'Gretel and Hansel'. But best of all, they gave powerful and varied roles to women while allowing men to be sensitive, in need of protection and rewarded for their kindness.

The book sparked some really interesting discussions with our editor, Louisa Joyner. From the offset she understood the power in the purity of the idea. We decided to be very strict and keep the text identical, except for the gender-swapped words. This did leave us with some slightly dated words, like 'durst' or 'spake', which reflect the era in which these stories were first written. It also made us very aware of the prevalence of heteronormativity in the relationships between the characters, which also reflects the eras in which these stories were written. (We shall have to make a different algorithm to solve that!)

But leaving the text untouched bar the gender swap meant that we couldn't influence the stories with our own prejudices or assumptions about how each character should act. While many people have rewritten fairy tales, no one has ever simply swapped the genders. We found this far more interesting, as it left the analysis of the new stories firmly in the hands of the readers.

Some of the gendered words were easy to switch – swapping 'man' to 'woman' or 'her' to 'his'. Then there were the words that we culturally associate with 'men' and 'women', such as names, titles and clothes. We decided to swap these too. We swapped 'Jack' to 'Jacqueline', 'Lord' to 'Lady' and 'dress' to 'suit'. While it would be nice for anyone of any gender to be named whatever they like and wear whatever they feel comfortable in, we thought this would get confusing. Instead we decided to simply swap our existing world, with all its binary ideas of what being a 'man' or 'woman' is, rather than create a utopian world where none of those labels mattered. We want this book to feel like it could be from a parallel universe, where women hold the power and always have.

The main complexity when gender-swapping text came when anything biological occurred, like sex or birth. Thankfully, as these are fairy tales, we only had to worry about the latter. There was much talk about if a man could bring a child into this world ('Perhaps he caught it coming out?') or if a magic rooster could lay an egg ('Why not – it's magic?'). We also had an interesting discussion around Rapunzel's hair. How could a twelve-year-old boy grow such a long beard? With the same magic, we imagine, that allows a twelve-year-old girl to grow such long hair.

Karrie: Once the text was swapped it was time for me to begin the illustrations. At first I felt a bit daunted, drawing these famous stories that had been illustrated to death. But I was confident that our gender swap would give me a new angle to approach them from. I began by researching classical paintings and illustrations of fairy tales and soon patterns began to emerge – the passive stances and exposed throats of the princesses; the clothes that seemed to cling to their bodies in some places, while simultaneously falling off them. I copied these drawings but swapped the genders round to see the effect. Following this research, I then began to draw my own gender-swapped versions, paying attention to the new power balance in each image. I also researched the origins of each fairy tale, from eighteenth-century France for 'Handsome and the Beast' to nineteenth-century Denmark for 'Thumbelin', drawing inspiration from the textiles and furniture of the countries and centuries in which the stories originated, but using brightly coloured palettes to give them a modern twist. I used watercolours and inks to paint them – my hands were a mess of colours for months on end until we finally finished the book.

We had so much fun making *Gender Swapped Fairy Tales*, but we also want it to explore serious questions. Our aim is no less than to illuminate and disrupt the gender stereotypes woven into the stories we've been told since childhood.

It already seems to be having an effect on our little family. Not so long ago, I showed our two-year-old daughter the 'Little Red Riding Hood' painting I had been working on in my studio earlier that day. In it a huge, big, bad lady-wolf towers over a little red-hooded boy. Our daughter was intrigued and studied it intensely. Later that night, while watching a David Attenborough documentary, I asked her: 'What animal would you like to be?' Without missing a beat, she answered: 'A big, bad wolf!'

We hope you find this to be a beautiful and thought-provoking book that shows you the world from a new point of view.

We'd love to hear your thoughts and observations, so do get in touch at genderswappedstories.com or on social media – @KarrieFransman and @JonPlackett.

Warmest wishes,
Karrie Fransman & Jonathan Plackett

GENDER SWAPPED
FAIRY TALES

HANDSOME AND
THE BEAST

Once upon a time, in a very far-off country, there lived a merchant who had been so fortunate in all her undertakings that she was enormously rich. As she had, however, six daughters and six sons, she found that her money was not too much to let them all have everything they fancied, as they were accustomed to do.

But one day a most unexpected misfortune befell them. Their house caught fire and was speedily burnt to the ground, with all the splendid furniture, the books, pictures, gold, silver, and precious goods it contained; and this was only the beginning of their troubles. Their mother, who had until this moment prospered in all ways, suddenly lost every ship she had upon the sea, either by dint of pirates, shipwreck, or fire. Then she heard that her clerks in distant countries, whom she trusted entirely, had proved unfaithful; and at last from great wealth she fell into the direst poverty.

All that she had left was a little house in a desolate place at least a hundred leagues from the town in which she had lived, and to this she was forced to retreat with her children, who were in despair at the idea of leading such a different life. Indeed, the sons at first hoped that their friends, who had been so numerous while they were rich, would insist on their staying in their houses now they no longer possessed one. But they soon found that they were left alone, and that their former friends even attributed their misfortunes to their own extravagance, and showed no intention of offering them any help. So nothing was left for them but to take their departure to the cottage, which stood in the midst of a dark forest, and seemed to be the most dismal place upon the face of the earth. As they were too poor to have any servants, the boys had to work hard, like peasants, and the daughters, for their part, cultivated the fields to earn their living. Roughly clothed, and living in the simplest way, the boys regretted unceasingly the luxuries and amusements of their former life; only the youngest tried to be brave and cheerful. He had been as sad as anyone when misfortune first overtook his mother, but, soon recovering his natural gaiety, he set to work to make the best of things, to amuse his mother and sisters as well as he could, and to try to persuade his brothers to join him in dancing and singing. But they would do nothing of the sort, and, because he was not as doleful as themselves, they declared that this miserable life was all he was fit for.

But he was really far prettier and cleverer than they were; indeed, he was so lovely that he was always called Handsome. After two years, when they were all beginning to get used to their new life, something happened to disturb their tranquillity. Their mother received the news that one of her ships, which she had believed to be lost, had come safely into port with a rich cargo. All the daughters and sons at once thought that their poverty was at an end, and wanted to set out directly for the town; but their mother, who was more prudent, begged them to wait a little, and, though it was harvest-time, and she could ill be spared, determined to go herself first, to make inquiries. Only the youngest son had any doubt but that they would soon again be as rich as they were before, or at least rich enough to live comfortably in some town where they would find amusement and gay companions once more. So they all loaded their mother with commissions for jewels and suits which it would have taken a fortune to buy; only Handsome, feeling sure that it was of no use, did not ask for anything. His mother, noticing his silence, said: "And what shall I bring for you, Handsome?"

"The only thing I wish for is to see you come home safely," he answered.

But this reply vexed his brothers, who fancied he was blaming them for having asked for such costly things. His mother, however, was pleased, but as she thought that at his age he certainly ought to like pretty presents, she told him to choose something.

"Well, dear mother," he said, "as you insist upon it, I beg that you will bring me a rose. I have not seen one since we came here, and I love them so much."

So the merchant set out and reached the town as quickly as possible, but only to find that her former companions, believing her to be dead, had divided between them the goods which the ship had brought; and after six months of trouble and expense she found herself as poor as when she started, having been able to recover only just enough to pay the cost of her journey. To make matters worse, she was obliged to leave the town in the most terrible weather, so that by the time she was within a few leagues of her home she was almost exhausted with cold and fatigue. Though she knew it would take some hours to get through the forest, she was so anxious to be at her journey's end that she resolved to go on; but night overtook her, and the deep snow and bitter frost made it impossible for her horse to carry her any further. Not a house was to be seen; the only shelter she could get was the hollow trunk of a great tree, and there she crouched all the night, which seemed to her the longest she had ever known. In spite of her weariness the howling of the wolves kept her awake, and even when at last the day broke she was not much better off, for the falling snow had covered up every path, and she did not know which way to turn.

At length she made out some sort of track, and though at the beginning it was so rough and slippery that she fell down more than once, it presently became easier, and led her into an avenue of trees, which ended in a splendid castle. It seemed to the merchant very strange that no snow had fallen in the avenue, which was entirely composed of orange trees, covered with flowers and fruit. When she reached the first court of the castle she saw before her a flight of agate steps, and went up them, and passed through several splendidly furnished rooms. The pleasant warmth of the air revived her, and she felt very hungry; but there seemed to be nobody in all this vast and splendid palace whom she could ask to give her something to eat. Deep silence reigned everywhere, and, at last, tired of roaming through empty rooms and galleries, she stopped in a room smaller than the rest, where a clear fire was burning and a couch was drawn up cosily close to it. Thinking that this must be prepared for someone who was expected, she sat down to wait till she should come, and very soon fell into a sweet sleep.

When her extreme hunger wakened her after several hours, she was still alone; but a little table, upon which was a good dinner, had been drawn up close to her, and, as she had eaten nothing for twenty-four hours, she lost no time in beginning her meal, hoping that she might soon have an opportunity of thanking her considerate entertainer, whoever it might be. But no one appeared, and even after another long sleep, from which she awoke completely refreshed, there was no sign of anybody, though a fresh meal of dainty cakes and fruit was prepared upon the little table at her elbow.

Being naturally timid, the silence began to terrify her, and she resolved to search once more through all the rooms; but it was of no use. Not even a servant was to be seen; there was no sign of life in the palace! She began to wonder what she should do, and to amuse herself by pretending that all the treasures she saw were her own, and considering how she would divide them among her children. Then she went down into the garden, and though it was winter everywhere else, here the sun shone, and the birds sang, and the flowers bloomed, and the air was soft and sweet. The merchant, in ecstasies with all she saw and heard, said to herself:

"All this must be meant for me. I will go this minute and bring my children to share all these delights."

In spite of being so cold and weary when she reached the castle, she had taken her horse to the stable and fed it. Now she thought she would saddle it for her homeward journey, and she turned down the path which led to the stable. This path had a hedge of roses on each side of it, and the merchant thought she had never seen or smelt such exquisite flowers. They reminded her of her promise to Handsome, and she stopped and had just gathered one to take to him when she was startled by a strange noise behind her. Turning round, she saw a frightful Beast, which seemed to be very angry and said, in a terrible voice:

"Who told you that you might gather my roses? Was it not enough that I allowed you to be in my palace and was kind to you? This is the way you show your gratitude, by stealing my flowers! But your insolence shall not go unpunished." The merchant, terrified by these furious words, dropped the fatal rose, and, throwing herself on her knees, cried: "Pardon me, noble ma'am. I am truly grateful to you for your hospitality, which was so magnificent that I could not imagine that you would be offended by my taking such a little thing as a rose." But the Beast's anger was not lessened by this speech.

"You are very ready with excuses and flattery," she cried; "but that will not save you from the death you deserve."

"Alas!" thought the merchant, "if my son Handsome could only know what danger his rose has brought me into!"

And in despair she began to tell the Beast all her misfortunes, and the reason of her journey, not forgetting to mention Handsome's request.

"A queen's ransom would hardly have procured all that my other sons asked," she said; "but I thought that I might at least take Handsome his rose. I beg you to forgive me, for you see I meant no harm."

The Beast considered for a moment, and then she said, in a less furious tone:

"I will forgive you on one condition – that is, that you will give me one of your sons."

"Ah!" cried the merchant, "if I were cruel enough to buy my own life at the expense of one of my children's, what excuse could I invent to bring him here?"

"No excuse would be necessary," answered the Beast. "If he comes at all he must come willingly. On no other condition will I have him. See if any one of them is courageous enough, and loves you well enough to come and save your life. You seem to be an honest woman, so I will trust you to go home. I give you a month to see if any of your sons will come back with you and stay here, to let you go free. If none of them is willing, you must come alone, after bidding them goodbye for ever, for then you will belong to me. And do not imagine that you can hide from me, for if you fail to keep your word I will come and fetch you!" added the Beast grimly.

The merchant accepted this proposal, though she did not really think any of her sons could be persuaded to come. She promised to return at the time appointed, and then, anxious to escape from the presence of the Beast, she asked permission to set off at once. But the Beast answered that she could not go until the next day.

"Then you will find a horse ready for you," she said. "Now go and eat your supper, and await my orders."

The poor merchant, more dead than alive, went back to her room, where the most delicious supper was already served on the little table, which was drawn up before a blazing fire. But she was too terrified to eat, and only tasted a few of the dishes, for fear the Beast should be angry if she did not obey her orders. When she had finished she heard a great noise in the next room, which she knew meant that the Beast was coming. As she could do nothing to escape her visit, the only thing that remained was to seem as little afraid as possible; so when the Beast appeared and asked roughly if she had supped well, the merchant answered humbly that she had, thanks to her host's kindness. Then the Beast warned her to remember their agreement, and to prepare her son exactly for what he had to expect.

"Do not get up tomorrow", she added, "until you see the sun and hear a golden bell ring. Then you will find your breakfast waiting for you here, and the horse you are to ride will be ready in the courtyard. She will also bring you back again when you come with your son a month hence. Farewell. Take a rose to Handsome, and remember your promise!"

The merchant was only too glad when the Beast went away, and though she could not sleep for sadness, she lay down until the sun rose. Then, after a hasty breakfast, she went to gather Handsome's rose, and mounted her horse, which carried her off so swiftly that in an instant she had lost sight of the palace, and she was still wrapped in gloomy thoughts when it stopped before the door of the cottage.

Her daughters and sons, who had been very uneasy at her long absence, rushed to meet her, eager to know the result of her journey, which, seeing her mounted upon a splendid horse and wrapped in a rich mantle, they supposed to be favourable. But she hid the truth from them at first, only saying sadly to Handsome as she gave him the rose:

"Here is what you asked me to bring you; you little know what it has cost."

But this excited their curiosity so greatly that presently she told them her adventures from beginning to end, and then they were all very unhappy. The boys lamented loudly over their lost hopes, and the daughters declared that their mother should not return to this terrible castle, and began to make plans for killing the Beast if it should come to fetch her. But she reminded them that she had promised to go back. Then the boys were very angry with Handsome, and said it was all his fault, and that if he had asked for something sensible this would never have happened, and complained bitterly that they should have to suffer for his folly.

Poor Handsome, much distressed, said to them:

"I have, indeed, caused this misfortune, but I assure you I did it innocently. Who could have guessed that to ask for a rose in the middle of summer would cause so much misery? But as I did the mischief it is only just that I should suffer for it. I will therefore go back with my mother to keep her promise."

At first nobody would hear of this arrangement, and his mother and sisters, who loved him dearly, declared that nothing should make them let him go; but Handsome was firm. As the time drew near he divided all his little possessions between his brothers, and said goodbye to everything he loved, and when the fatal day came he encouraged and cheered his mother as they mounted together the horse which had brought her back. It seemed to fly rather than gallop, but so smoothly that Handsome was not frightened; indeed, he would have enjoyed the journey if he had not feared what might happen to him at the end of it. His mother still tried to persuade him to go back, but in vain. While they were talking the night fell, and then, to their great surprise, wonderful coloured lights began to shine in all directions, and splendid fireworks blazed out before them; all the forest was illuminated by them, and even felt pleasantly warm, though it had been bitterly cold before. This lasted until they reached the avenue of orange trees, where were statues holding flaming torches, and when they got nearer to the palace they saw that it was illuminated from the roof to the ground, and music sounded softly from the courtyard. "The Beast must be very hungry", said Handsome, trying to laugh, "if she makes all this rejoicing over the arrival of her prey."

But, in spite of his anxiety, he could not help admiring all the wonderful things he saw.

The horse stopped at the foot of the flight of steps leading to the terrace, and when they had dismounted his mother led him to the little room she had been in before, where they found a splendid fire burning, and the table daintily spread with a delicious supper.

The merchant knew that this was meant for them, and Handsome, who was rather less frightened now that he had passed through so many rooms and seen nothing of the Beast, was quite willing to begin, for his long ride had made him very hungry. But they had hardly finished their meal when the noise of the Beast's footsteps was heard approaching, and Handsome clung to his mother in terror, which became all the greater when he saw how frightened she was. But when the Beast really appeared, though he trembled at the sight of her, he made a great effort to hide his horror, and saluted her respectfully.

This evidently pleased the Beast. After looking at him she said, in a tone that might have struck terror into the boldest heart, though she did not seem to be angry:

"Good evening, old woman. Good evening, Handsome."

The merchant was too terrified to reply, but Handsome answered sweetly: "Good evening, Beast."

"Have you come willingly?" asked the Beast. "Will you be content to stay here when your mother goes away?"

Handsome answered bravely that he was quite prepared to stay.

"I am pleased with you," said the Beast. "As you have come of your own accord, you may stay. As for you, old woman," she added, turning to the merchant, "at sunrise tomorrow you will take your departure. When the bell rings get up quickly and eat your breakfast, and you will find the same horse waiting to take you home; but remember that you must never expect to see my palace again."

Then turning to Handsome, she said:

"Take your mother into the next room, and help her to choose everything you think your sisters and brothers would like to have. You will find two travelling trunks there; fill them as full as you can. It is only just that you should send them something very precious as a remembrance of yourself."

Then she went away, after saying: "Goodbye, Handsome; goodbye, old woman"; and though Handsome was beginning to think with great dismay of his mother's departure, he was afraid to disobey the Beast's orders; and they went into the next room, which had shelves and cupboards all round it. They were greatly surprised at the riches it contained. There were splendid suits fit for a king, with all the ornaments that were to be worn with them; and when Handsome opened the cupboards he was quite dazzled by the gorgeous jewels that lay in heaps upon every shelf. After choosing a vast quantity, which he divided between his brothers – for he had made a heap of the wonderful suits for each of them – he opened the last chest, which was full of gold.

"I think, Mother," he said, "that as the gold will be more useful to you, we had better take out the other things again, and fill the trunks with it." So they did this; but the more they put in, the more room there seemed to be, and at last they put back all the jewels and suits they had taken out, and Handsome even added as many more of the jewels as he could carry at once; and then the trunks were not too full, but they were so heavy that an elephant could not have carried them!

"The Beast was mocking us," cried the merchant; "she must have pretended to give us all these things, knowing that I could not carry them away."

"Let us wait and see," answered Handsome. "I cannot believe that she meant to deceive us. All we can do is to fasten them up and leave them ready."

So they did this and returned to the little room, where, to their astonishment, they found breakfast ready. The merchant ate hers with a good appetite, as the Beast's generosity made her believe that she might perhaps venture to come back soon and see Handsome. But he felt sure that his mother was leaving him for ever, so he was very sad when the bell rang sharply for the second time, and warned them that the time had come for them to part. They went down into the courtyard, where two horses were waiting, one loaded with the two trunks, the other for her to ride. They were pawing the ground in their impatience to start, and the merchant was forced to bid Handsome a hasty farewell; and as soon as she was mounted she went off at such a pace that he lost sight of her in an instant. Then Handsome began to cry, and wandered sadly back to his own room. But he soon found that he was very sleepy, and as he had nothing better to do he lay down and instantly fell asleep. And then he dreamed that he was walking by a brook bordered with trees, and lamenting his sad fate, when a young princess, handsomer than anyone he had ever seen, and with a voice that went straight to his heart, came and said to him: "Ah, Handsome! you are not so unfortunate as you suppose. Here you will be rewarded for all you have suffered elsewhere. Your every wish shall be gratified. Only try to find me out, no matter how I may be disguised, as I love you dearly, and in making me happy you will find your own happiness. Be as true-hearted as you are beautiful, and we shall have nothing left to wish for."

"What can I do, Princess, to make you happy?" said Handsome.

"Only be grateful," she answered, "and do not trust too much to your eyes. And, above all, do not desert me until you have saved me from my cruel misery."

After this he thought he found himself in a room with a stately and beautiful gentleman, who said to him:

"Dear Handsome, try not to regret all you have left behind you, for you are destined to a better fate. Only do not let yourself be deceived by appearances."

Handsome found his dreams so interesting that he was in no hurry to awake, but presently the clock roused him by calling his name softly twelve times, and then he got up and found his dressing table set out with everything he could possibly want; and when his toilet was finished he found dinner was waiting in the room next to his. But dinner does not take very long when you are all by yourself, and very soon he sat down cosily in the corner of a sofa, and began to think about the charming Princess he had seen in his dream.

"She said I could make her happy," said Handsome to himself.

"It seems, then, that this horrible Beast keeps her a prisoner. How can I set her free? I wonder why they both told me not to trust to appearances? I don't understand it. But, after all, it was only a dream, so why should I trouble myself about it? I had better go and find something to do to amuse myself."

So he got up and began to explore some of the many rooms of the palace.

The first he entered was lined with mirrors, and Handsome saw himself reflected on every side, and thought he had never seen such a charming room. Then a bracelet which was hanging from a chandelier caught his eye, and on taking it down he was greatly surprised to find that it held a portrait of his unknown admirer, just as he had seen her in his dream. With great delight he slipped the bracelet on his arm, and went on into a gallery of pictures, where he soon found a portrait of the same beautiful Princess, as large as life, and so well painted that as he studied it she seemed to smile kindly at him. Tearing himself away from the portrait at last, he passed through into a room which contained every musical instrument under the sun, and here he amused himself for a long while in trying some of them, and singing until he was tired. The next room was a library, and he saw everything he had ever wanted to read, as well as everything he had read, and it seemed to him that a whole lifetime would not be enough to even read the names of the books,

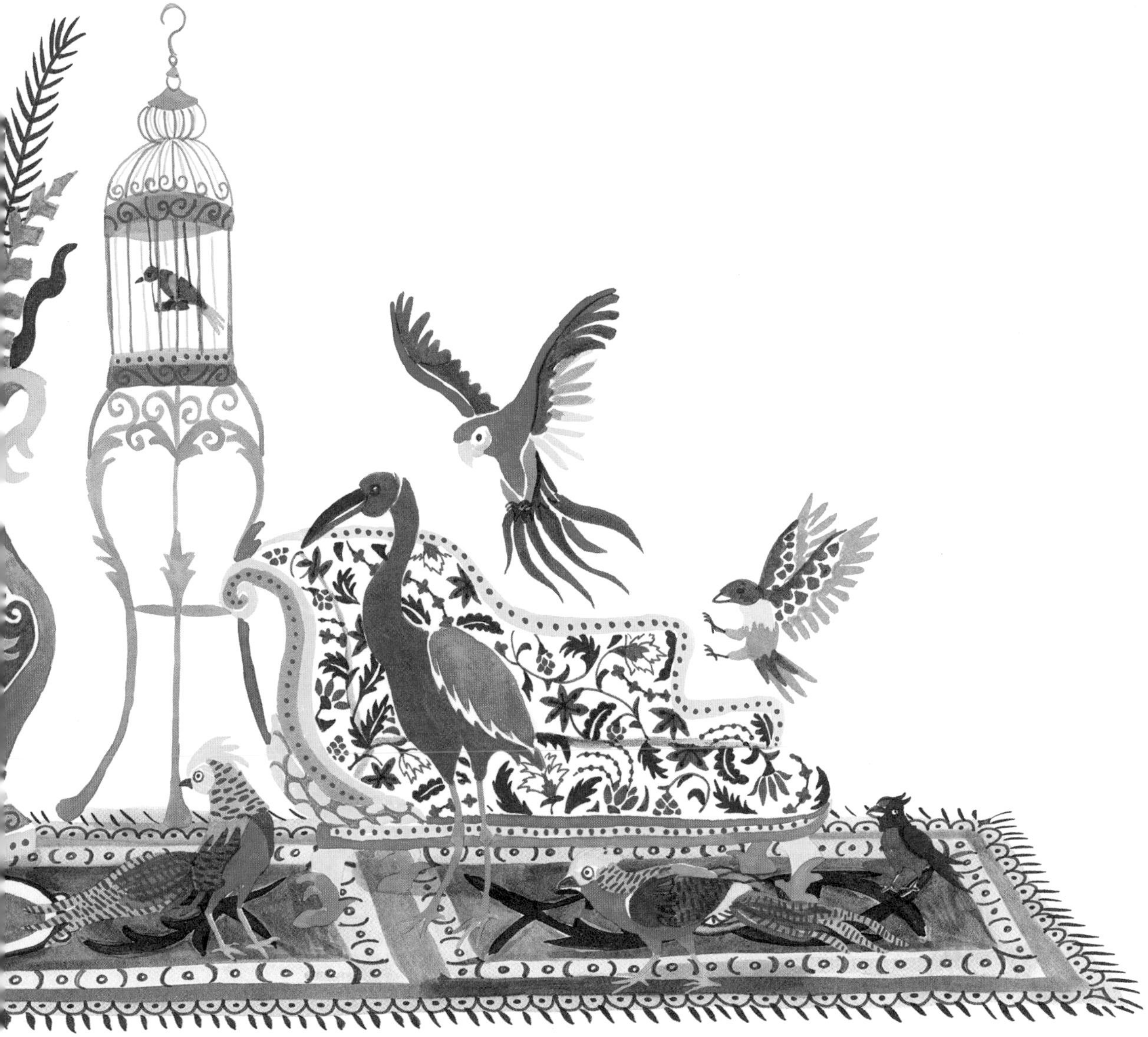

there were so many. By this time it was growing dusk, and wax candles in diamond and ruby candlesticks were beginning to light themselves in every room.

Handsome found his supper served just at the time he preferred to have it, but he did not see anyone or hear a sound, and, though his mother had warned him that he would be alone, he began to find it rather dull.

But presently he heard the Beast coming, and wondered tremblingly if she meant to eat him up now.

However, as she did not seem at all ferocious, and only said gruffly:

"Good evening, Handsome," he answered cheerfully and managed to conceal his terror. Then the Beast asked him how he had been amusing himself, and he told her all the rooms he had seen.

Then she asked if he thought he could be happy in her palace; and Handsome answered that everything was so beautiful that he would be very hard to please if he could not be happy. And after about an hour's talk Handsome began to think that the Beast was not nearly so terrible as he had supposed at first. Then she got up to leave him, and said in her gruff voice:

"Do you love me, Handsome? Will you marry me?"

"Oh! what shall I say?" cried Handsome, for he was afraid to make the Beast angry by refusing.

"Say 'yes' or 'no' without fear," she replied.

"Oh! no, Beast," said Handsome hastily.

"Since you will not, good night, Handsome," she said. And he answered:

"Good night, Beast," very glad to find that his refusal had not provoked her. And after she was gone he was very soon in bed and asleep, and dreaming of his unknown Princess. He thought she came and said to him:

"Ah, Handsome! why are you so unkind to me? I fear I am fated to be unhappy for many a long day still."

And then his dreams changed, but the charming Princess figured in them all; and when morning came his first thought was to look at the portrait, and see if it was really like her, and he found that it certainly was.

This morning he decided to amuse himself in the garden, for the sun shone, and all the fountains were playing; but he was astonished to find that every place was familiar to him, and presently he came to the brook where the myrtle trees were growing where he had first met the Princess in his dream, and that made him think more than ever that she must be kept a prisoner by the Beast. When he was tired he went back to the palace, and found a new room full of materials for every kind of work – ribbons to make into bows, and silks to work into flowers. Then there was an aviary full of rare birds, which were so tame that they flew to Handsome as soon as they saw him, and perched upon his shoulders and his head.

"Pretty little creatures," he said, "how I wish that your cage was nearer to my room, that I might often hear you sing!"

So saying he opened a door, and found to his delight that it led into his own room, though he had thought it was quite the other side of the palace.

There were more birds in a room farther on, parrots and cockatoos that could talk, and they greeted Handsome by name; indeed, he found them so entertaining that he took one or two back to his room, and they talked to him while he was at supper; after which the Beast paid him her usual visit, and asked the same questions as before, and then with a gruff "good night" she took her departure, and Handsome went to bed to dream of his mysterious Princess. The days passed swiftly in different amusements, and after a while Handsome found out another strange thing in the palace, which often pleased him when he was tired of being alone. There was one room which he had not noticed particularly; it was empty, except that under each of the windows stood a very comfortable chair; and the first time he had looked out of the window it had seemed to him that a black curtain prevented him from seeing anything outside. But the second time he went into the room, happening to be tired, he sat down in one of the chairs, when instantly the curtain was rolled aside, and a most amusing pantomime was acted before him; there were dances, and coloured lights, and music, and pretty suits, and it was all so gay that Handsome was in ecstasies. After that he tried the other seven windows in turn, and there was some new and surprising entertainment to be seen from each of them, so that Handsome never could feel lonely any more. Every evening after supper the Beast came to see him, and always before saying good night asked him in her terrible voice:

"Handsome, will you marry me?"

And it seemed to Handsome, now he understood her better, that when he said, "No, Beast," she went away quite sad. But his happy dreams of the beautiful young Princess soon made him forget the poor Beast, and the only thing that at all disturbed him was to be constantly told to distrust appearances, to let his heart guide him, and not his eyes, and many other equally perplexing things, which, consider as he would, he could not understand.

So everything went on for a long time, until at last, happy as he was, Handsome began to long for the sight of his mother and his sisters and brothers; and one night, seeing him look very sad, the Beast asked him what was the matter. Handsome had quite ceased to be afraid of her. Now he knew that she was really gentle in spite of her ferocious looks and her dreadful voice. So he answered that he was longing to see his home once more. Upon hearing this, the Beast seemed sadly distressed, and cried miserably.

"Ah! Handsome, have you the heart to desert an unhappy Beast like this? What more do you want to make you happy? Is it because you hate me that you want to escape?"

"No, dear Beast," answered Handsome softly, "I do not hate you, and I should be very sorry never to see you any more, but I long to see my mother again. Only let me go for two months, and I promise to come back to you and stay for the rest of my life."

The Beast, who had been sighing dolefully while he spoke, now replied:

"I cannot refuse you anything you ask, even though it should cost me my life. Take the four boxes you will find in the room next to your own, and fill them with everything you wish to take with you. But remember your promise and come back when the two months are over, or you may have cause to repent it, for if you do not come in good time you will find your faithful Beast dead. You will not need any chariot to bring you back. Only say goodbye to all your sisters and brothers the night before you come away, and when you have gone to bed turn this ring round upon your finger and say firmly: 'I wish to go back to my palace and see my Beast again.' Good night, Handsome. Fear nothing, sleep peacefully, and before long you shall see your mother once more."

As soon as Handsome was alone he has-tened to fill the boxes with all the rare and precious things he saw about him, and only when he was tired of heaping things into them did they seem to be full.

Then he went to bed, but could hardly sleep for joy. And when at last he did begin to dream of his beloved Princess he was grieved to see her stretched upon a grassy bank, sad and weary, and hardly like herself.

"What is the matter?" he cried.

But she looked at him reproachfully, and said:

"How can you ask me, cruel one? Are you not leaving me to my death perhaps?"

"Ah! don't be so sorrowful," cried Handsome; "I am only going to assure my mother that I am safe and happy. I have promised the Beast faithfully that I will come back, and she would die of grief if I did not keep my word!"

"What would that matter to you?" said the Princess. "Surely you would not care?"

"Indeed, I should be ungrateful if I did not care for such a kind Beast," cried Handsome indignantly. "I would die to save her from pain. I assure you it is not her fault that she is so ugly."

Just then a strange sound woke him – someone was speaking not very far away; and opening his eyes he found himself in a room he had never seen before, which was certainly not nearly so splendid as those he was used to in the Beast's palace. Where could he be? He got up and dressed hastily, and then saw that the boxes he had packed the night before were all in the room. While he was wondering by what magic the Beast had transported them and himself to this strange place he suddenly heard his mother's voice, and rushed out and greeted her joyfully. His sisters and brothers were all astonished at his appearance, as they had never expected to see him again, and there was no end to the questions they asked him. He had also much to hear about what had happened to them while he was away, and of his mother's journey home. But when they heard that he had only come to be with them for a short time, and then must go back to the Beast's palace for ever, they lamented loudly. Then Handsome asked his mother what she thought could be the meaning of his strange dreams, and why the Princess constantly begged him not to trust to appearances. After much consideration, she answered: "You tell me yourself that the Beast, frightful as she is, loves you dearly, and deserves your love and gratitude for her gentleness and kindness; I think the Princess must mean you to understand that you ought to reward her by doing as she wishes you to, in spite of her ugliness."

Handsome could not help seeing that this seemed very probable; still, when he thought of his dear Princess who was so beautiful, he did not feel at all inclined to marry the Beast. At any rate, for two months he need not decide, but could enjoy himself with his brothers. But though they were rich now, and lived in town again, and had plenty of acquaintances, Handsome found that nothing amused him very much; and he often thought of the palace, where he was so happy, especially as at home he never once dreamed of his dear Princess, and he felt quite sad without her.

Then his brothers seemed to have got quite used to being without him, and even found him rather in the way, so he would not have been sorry when the two months were over but for his mother and sisters, who begged him to stay, and seemed so grieved at the thought of his departure that he had not the courage to say goodbye to them. Every day when he got up he meant to say it at night, and when night came he put it off again, until at last he had a dismal dream which helped him to make up his mind. He thought he was wandering in a lonely path in the palace gardens, when he heard groans which seemed to come from some bushes hiding the entrance of a cave, and running quickly to see what could be the matter, he found the Beast stretched out upon her side, apparently dying. She reproached him faintly with being the cause of her distress, and at the same moment a stately gentleman appeared, and said very gravely:

"Ah! Handsome, you are only just in time to save her life. See what happens when people do not keep their promises! If you had delayed one day more, you would have found her dead."

Handsome was so terrified by this dream that the next morning he announced his intention of going back at once, and that very night he said goodbye to his mother and all his sisters and brothers, and as soon as he was in bed he turned his ring round upon his finger, and said firmly:

"I wish to go back to my palace and see my Beast again," as he had been told to do.

Then he fell asleep instantly, and only woke up to hear the clock saying, "Handsome, Handsome," twelve times in its musical voice, which told him at once that he was really in the palace once more. Everything was just as before, and his birds were so glad to see him! But Handsome thought he had never known such a long day, for he was so anxious to see the Beast again that he felt as if supper-time would never come.

But when it did come and no Beast appeared he was really frightened; so, after listening and waiting for a long time, he ran down into the garden to search for her. Up and down the paths and avenues ran poor Handsome, calling her in vain, for no one answered, and not a trace of her could he find; until at last, quite tired, he stopped for a minute's rest, and saw that he was standing opposite the shady path he had seen in his dream. He rushed down it, and, sure enough, there was the cave, and in it lay the Beast – asleep, as Handsome thought. Quite glad to have found her, he ran up and stroked her head, but, to his horror, she did not move or open her eyes.

"Oh! she is dead; and it is all my fault," said Handsome, crying bitterly.

But then, looking at her again, he fancied she still breathed, and, hastily fetching some water from the nearest fountain, he sprinkled it over her face, and, to his great delight, she began to revive.

"Oh! Beast, how you frightened me!" he cried. "I never knew how much I loved you until just now, when I feared I was too late to save your life."

"Can you really love such an ugly creature as I am?" said the Beast faintly. "Ah! Handsome, you only came just in time. I was dying because I thought you had forgotten your promise. But go back now and rest, I shall see you again by-and-by."

Handsome, who had half expected that she would be angry with him, was reassured by her gentle voice, and went back to the palace, where supper was awaiting him; and afterwards the Beast came in as usual, and talked about the time he had spent with his mother, asking if he had enjoyed himself, and if they had all been very glad to see him.

Handsome answered politely, and quite enjoyed telling her all that had happened to him. And when at last the time came for her to go, and she asked, as she had so often asked before, "Handsome, will you marry me?" he answered softly:

"Yes, dear Beast."

As he spoke a blaze of light sprang up before the windows of the palace; fireworks crackled and guns banged, and across the avenue of orange trees, in letters all made of fire-flies, was written: "Long live the Princess and her Groom."

Turning to ask the Beast what it could all mean, Handsome found that she had disappeared, and in her place stood his long-loved Princess! At the same moment the wheels of a chariot were heard upon the terrace, and two gentlemen entered the room. One of them Handsome recognized as the stately gentleman he had seen in his dreams; the other was also so grand and kingly that Handsome hardly knew which to greet first.

But the one he already knew said to his companion:

"Well, King, this is Handsome, who has had the courage to rescue your daughter from the terrible enchantment. They love one another, and only your consent to their marriage is wanting to make them perfectly happy."

"I consent with all my heart," cried the King. "How can I ever thank you enough, charming boy, for having restored my dear daughter to her natural form?"

And then he tenderly embraced Handsome and the Princess, who had meanwhile been greeting the Fairy and receiving his congratulations.

"Now," said the Fairy to Handsome, "I suppose you would like me to send for all your sisters and brothers to dance at your wedding?"

And so he did, and the marriage was celebrated the very next day with the utmost splendour, and Handsome and the Princess lived happily ever after.

CINDER, OR THE LITTLE GLASS SLIPPER

Once there was a lady who married, for her second husband, the proudest and most haughty man that was ever seen. He had, by a former wife, two sons of his own humour, who were, indeed, exactly like him in all things. She had likewise, by another husband, a young son, but of unparalleled goodness and sweetness of temper, which he took from his father, who was the best creature in the world.

No sooner were the ceremonies of the wedding over but the stepfather began to show himself in his true colours. He could not bear the good qualities of this pretty boy, and the less because they made his own sons appear the more odious. He employed him in the meanest work of the house: he scoured the dishes, tables, etc., and scrubbed sir's chamber, and those of the masters, his sons; he lay up in a sorry garret, upon a wretched straw bed, while his brothers lay in fine rooms, with floors all inlaid, upon beds of the very newest fashion, and where they had looking glasses so large that they might see themselves at their full length from head to foot.

The poor boy bore all patiently, and dared not tell his mother, who would have rattled him off; for her husband governed her entirely. When he had done his work, he used to go into the chimney corner, and sit down among cinders and ashes, which made him commonly be called Cinderboy; but the youngest, who was not so rude and uncivil as the eldest, called him Cinder. However, Cinder, notwithstanding his mean apparel, was a hundred times handsomer than his brothers, though they were always dressed very richly.

It happened that the Queen's daughter gave a ball, and invited all persons of fashion to it. Our young masters were also invited, for they cut a very grand figure among the quality. They were mightily delighted at this invitation, and wonderfully busy in choosing out such gowns, pantaloons, and head-clothes as might become them. This was a new trouble to Cinder; for it was he who ironed his brothers' linen, and plaited their ruffles; they talked all day long of nothing but how they should be dressed.

"For my part," said the eldest, "I will wear my red velvet suit with French trimming."

"And I", said the youngest, "shall have my usual pantaloons; but then, to make amends for that, I will put on my gold-flowered cloak, and my diamond chest-piece, which is far from being the most ordinary one in the world."

They sent for the best tire-man they could get to make up their head-dresses and adjust their neckerchiefs, and they had their red brushes and patches from Monsieur de la Poche.

Cinder was likewise called up to them to be consulted in all these matters, for he had excellent notions, and advised them always for the best, nay, and offered his services to dress their heads, which they were very willing he should do. As he was doing this, they said to him:

"Cinder, would you not be glad to go to the ball?"

"Alas!" said he, "you only jeer me; it is not for such as I am to go thither."

"Thou art in the right of it," replied they; "it would make the people laugh to see a Cinderboy at a ball."

Anyone but Cinder would have dressed their heads awry, but he was very good, and dressed them perfectly well. They were almost two days without eating, so much were they transported with joy. They broke above a dozen laces in trying to be laced up close, that they might have a fine slender shape, and they were continually at their looking glasses. At last the happy day came; they went to Court, and Cinder followed them with his eyes as long as he could, and when he had lost sight of them, he fell a-crying.

His godfather, who saw him all in tears, asked him what was the matter.

"I wish I could – I wish I could – he was not able to speak the rest, being interrupted by his tears and sobbing.

This godfather of his, who was a fairy, said to him, "Thou wishest thou couldst go to the ball; is it not so?"

"Y—es," cried Cinder, with a great sigh.

"Well," said his godfather, "be but a good boy, and I will contrive that thou shalt go." Then he took him into his chamber, and said to him, "Run into the garden, and bring me a pumpkin."

Cinder went immediately to gather the finest he could get, and brought it to his godfather, not being able to imagine how this pumpkin could make him go to the ball. His godfather scooped out all the inside of it, having left nothing but the rind; which done, he struck it with his wand, and the pumpkin was instantly turned into a fine coach, gilded all over with gold.

He then went to look into his mousetrap, where he found six mice, all alive, and ordered Cinder to lift up a little the trapdoor, when, giving each mouse, as it went out, a little tap with his wand, the mouse was that moment turned into a fine horse, which altogether made a very fine set of six horses of a beautiful mouse-coloured dapple-grey. Being at a loss for a coachwoman,

"I will go and see," says Cinder, "if there is never a rat in the rat trap – we may make a coachwoman of her."

"Thou art in the right," replied his godfather; "go and look."

Cinder brought the trap to him, and in it there were three huge rats. The fairy made choice of one of the three which had the longest fur, and, having touched her with his wand, she was turned into a fat, jolly coachwoman, who had the smartest whiskers eyes ever beheld. After that, he said to him:

"Go again into the garden, and you will find six lizards behind the watering-pot; bring them to me."

He had no sooner done so but his godfather turned them into six footwomen, who skipped up immediately behind the coach, with their liveries all bedaubed with gold and silver, and clung as close behind each other as if they had done nothing else their whole lives. The Fairy then said to Cinder:

"Well, you see here an equipage fit to go to the ball with; are you not pleased with it?"

"Oh! yes," cried he; "but must I go thither as I am, in these nasty rags?"

His godfather only just touched him with his wand, and, at the same instant, his clothes were turned into cloth of gold and silver, all beset with jewels. This done, he gave him a pair of glass slippers, the prettiest in the whole world. Being thus decked out, he got up into his coach; but his godfather, above all things, commanded him not to stay till after midnight, telling him, at the same time, that if he stayed one moment longer, the coach would be a pumpkin again, his horses mice, his coachwoman a rat, his footwomen lizards, and his clothes become just as they were before.

He promised his godfather he would not fail of leaving the ball before midnight; and then away he drives, scarce able to contain himself for joy. The Queen's daughter, who was told that a great prince, whom nobody knew, was come, ran out to receive him; she gave him her hand as he alighted out of the coach, and led him into the hall, among all the company. There was immediately a profound silence, they left off dancing, and the violins ceased to play, so attentive was everyone to contemplate the singular beauties of the unknown newcomer. Nothing was then heard but a confused noise of:

"Ha! how handsome he is! Ha! how handsome he is!"

The Queen herself, old as she was, could not help watching him, and telling the King softly that it was a long time since she had seen so beautiful and lovely a creature.

All the gentlemen were busied in considering his clothes and headdress, that they might have some made next day after the same pattern, provided they could meet with such fine materials and as able hands to make them.

The Queen's daughter conducted him to the most honourable seat, and afterwards took him out to dance with her; he danced so very gracefully that they all more and more admired him. A fine collation was served up, whereof the young princess ate not a morsel, so intently was she busied in gazing on him.

He went and sat down by his brothers, showing them a thousand civilities, giving them part of the oranges and citrons which the Princess had presented him with, which very much surprised them, for they did not know him. While Cinder was thus amusing his brothers, he heard the clock strike eleven and three-quarters, whereupon he immediately made a courtesy to the company and hasted away as fast as he could.

Being got home, he ran to seek out his godfather, and, after having thanked him, he said he could not but heartily wish he might go next day to the ball, because the Queen's daughter had desired him.

As he was eagerly telling his godfather whatever had passed at the ball, his two brothers knocked at the door, which Cinder ran and opened.

"How long you have stayed!" cried he, gaping, rubbing his eyes and stretching himself as if he had been just waked out of his sleep; he had not, however, any manner of inclination to sleep since they went from home.

"If thou hadst been at the ball," said one of his brothers, "thou wouldst not have been tired with it. There came thither the finest prince, the most beautiful ever was seen with mortal eyes; he showed us a thousand civilities, and gave us oranges and citrons."

Cinder seemed very indifferent in the matter; indeed, he asked them the name of that prince; but they told him they did not know it, and that the Queen's daughter was very uneasy on his account and would give all the world to know who he was. At this Cinder, smiling, replied:

"He must, then, be very beautiful indeed; how happy you have been! Could not I see him? Ah! dear Mr Charles, do lend me your yellow suit of clothes which you wear every day."

"Ay, to be sure!" cried Mr Charles; "lend my clothes to such a dirty Cinderboy as thou art! I should be a fool."

Cinder, indeed, expected well such answer, and was very glad of the refusal; for he would have been sadly put to it if his brother had lent him what he asked for jestingly.

The next day the two brothers were at the ball, and so was Cinder, but dressed more magnificently than before. The Queen's daughter was always by him, and never ceased her compliments and kind speeches to him; to whom all this was so far from being tiresome that he quite forgot what his godfather had recommended to him; so that he, at last, counted the clock striking twelve when he took it to be no more than eleven; he then rose up and fled, as nimble as a deer. The Princess followed, but could not overtake him. He left behind one of his glass slippers, which the Princess took up most carefully. He got home but quite out of breath, and in his nasty old clothes, having nothing left him of all his finery but one of the little slippers, fellow to that he dropped. The guards at the palace gate were asked:

If they had not seen a prince go out.

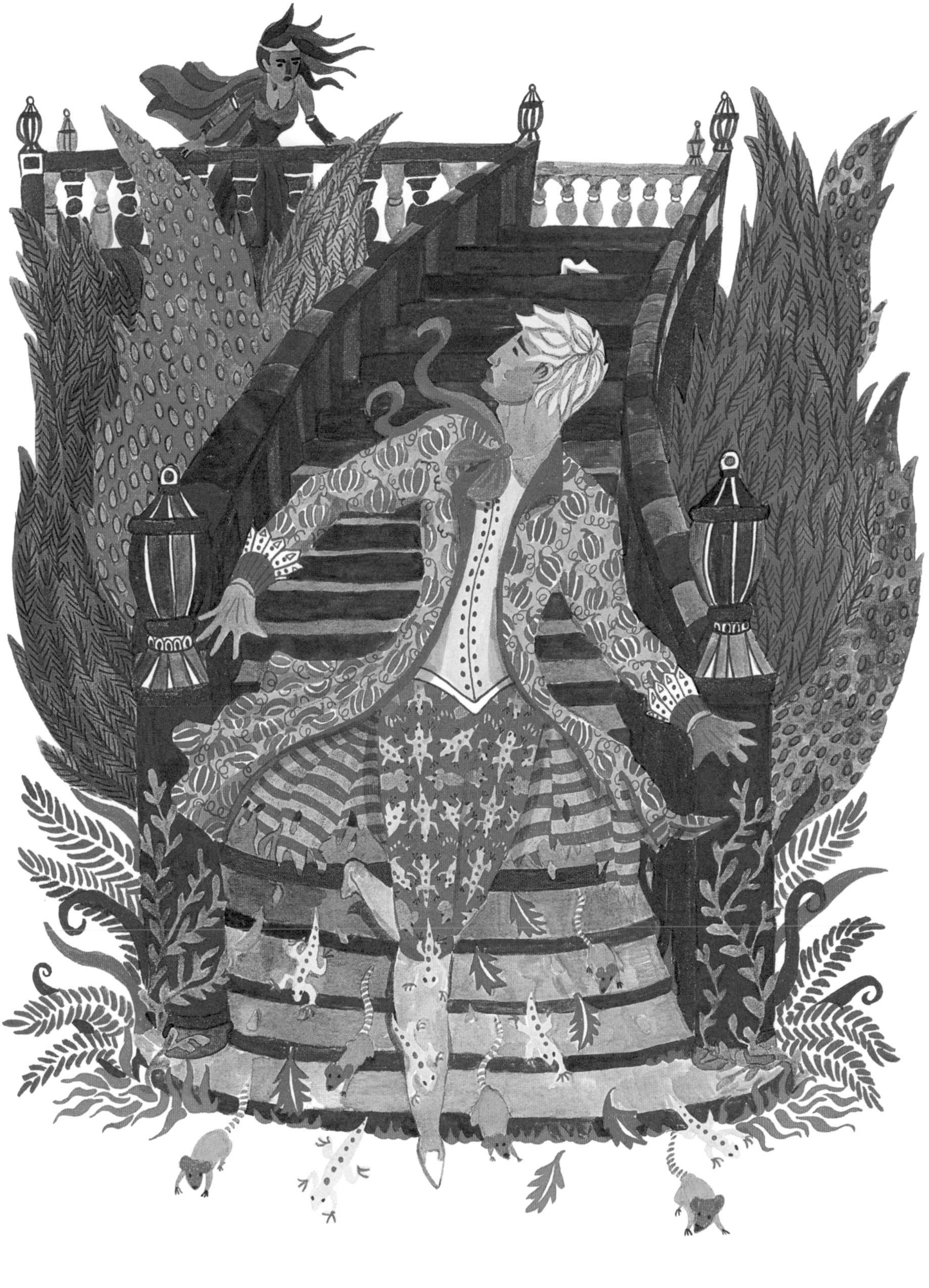

Who said: They had seen nobody go out but a young boy, very meanly dressed, and who had more the air of a poor country lad than a gentleman.

When the two brothers returned from the ball Cinder asked them: If they had been well diverted, and if the fine gentleman had been there.

They told him: Yes, but that he hurried away immediately when it struck twelve, and with so much haste that he dropped one of his little glass slippers, the prettiest in the world, which the Queen's daughter had taken up; that she had done nothing but look at him all the time at the ball, and that most certainly she was very much in love with the beautiful person who owned the glass slipper.

What they said was very true; for a few days after the Queen's daughter caused it to be proclaimed, by sound of trumpet, that she would marry him whose foot the slipper would just fit. They whom she employed began to try it upon the princes, then the dukes and all the Court, but in vain; it was brought to the two brothers, who did all they possibly could to thrust their foot into the slipper, but they could not effect it. Cinder, who saw all this, and knew his slipper, said to them, laughing:

"Let me see if it will not fit me."

His brothers burst out a-laughing, and began to banter him. The lady who was sent to try the slipper looked earnestly at Cinder, and, finding him very handsome, said:

44

It was but just that he should try, and that she had orders to let everyone make trial.

She obliged Cinder to sit down, and, putting the slipper to his foot, she found it went on very easily, and fitted him as if it had been made of wax. The astonishment his two brothers were in was excessively great, but still abundantly greater when Cinder pulled out of his pocket the other slipper, and put it on his foot. Thereupon, in came his godfather, who, having touched with his wand Cinder's clothes, made them richer and more magnificent than any of those he had before.

And now his two brothers found him to be that fine, beautiful gentleman whom they had seen at the ball. They threw themselves at his feet to beg pardon for all the ill-treatment they had made him undergo. Cinder took them up, and, as he embraced them, cried:

That he forgave them with all his heart, and desired them always to love him.

He was conducted to the young Princess, dressed as he was; she thought him more charming than ever, and, a few days after, married him. Cinder, who was no less good than beautiful, gave his two brothers lodgings in the palace, and that very same day matched them with two great ladies of the Court.

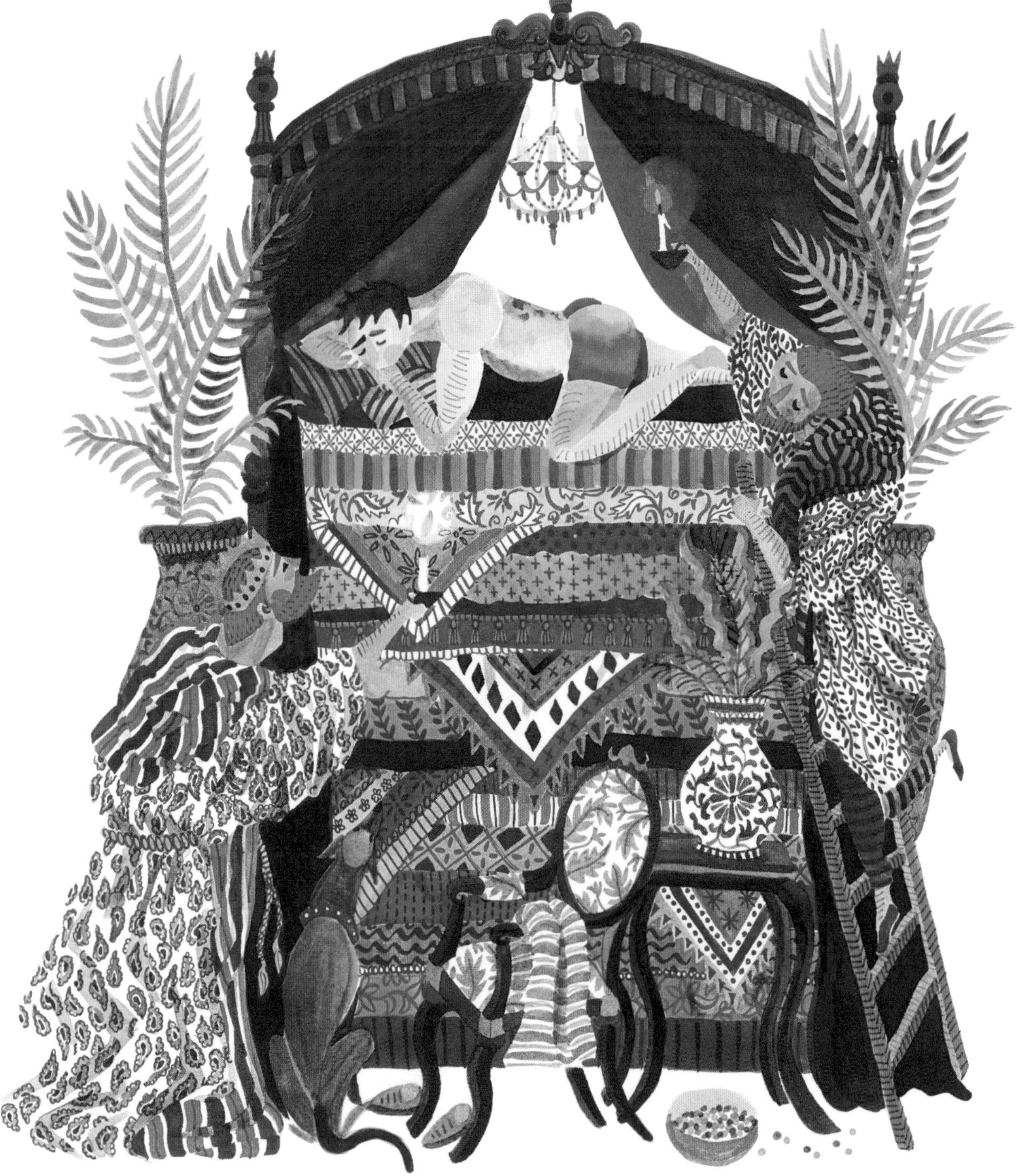

HOW TO TELL A
TRUE PRINCE

There was once upon a time a Princess who wanted to marry a Prince, but he must be a true Prince. So she travelled through the whole world to find one, but there was always something against each. There were plenty of Princes, but she could not find out if they were true Princes. In every case there was some little defect, which showed the genuine article was not yet found. So she came home again in very low spirits, for she had wanted very much to have a true Prince. One night there was a dreadful storm; it thundered and lightened and the rain streamed down in torrents. It was fearful! There was a knocking heard at the palace gate, and the old Queen went to open it.

There stood a Prince outside the gate; but oh, in what a sad plight he was from the rain and the storm! The water was running down from his hair and his trousers into the points of his shoes and out at the heels again. And yet he said he was a true Prince!

"Well, we shall soon find that!" thought the old King. But he said nothing, and went into the sleeping-room, took off all the bed-clothes, and laid a pea on the bottom of the bed. Then he put twenty mattresses on top of the pea, and twenty eider-down quilts on the top of the mattresses. And this was the bed in which the Prince was to sleep.

The next morning he was asked how he had slept.

"Oh, very badly!" said the Prince. "I scarcely closed my eyes all night! I am sure I don't know what was in the bed. I laid on something so hard that my whole body is black and blue. It is dreadful!"

Now they perceived that he was a true Prince, because he had felt the pea through the twenty mattresses and the twenty eider-down quilts.

No one but a true Prince could be so sensitive.

So the Princess married him, for now she knew that at last she had got hold of a true Prince. And the pea was put into the Royal Museum, where it is still to be seen if no one has stolen it. Now this is a true story.

JACQUELINE AND THE
BEANSTALK

Once upon a time there was a poor widower who lived in a little cottage with his only daughter Jacqueline.

Jacqueline was a giddy, thoughtless girl, but very kind-hearted and affectionate. There had been a hard winter, and after it the poor man had suffered from fever and ague. Jacqueline did no work as yet, and by degrees they grew dreadfully poor. The widower saw that there was no means of keeping Jacqueline and himself from starvation but by selling his cow; so one morning he said to his daughter, "I am too weak to go myself, Jacqueline, so you must take the cow to market for me, and sell him."

Jacqueline liked going to market to sell the cow very much; but as she was on the way, she met a butcher who had some beautiful beans in her hand. Jacqueline stopped to look at them, and the butcher told the girl that they were of great value, and persuaded the silly girl to sell the cow for these beans.

When she brought them home to her father instead of the money he expected for his nice cow, he was very vexed and shed many tears, scolding Jacqueline for her folly. She was very sorry, and father and daughter went to bed very sadly that night; their last hope seemed gone.

At daybreak Jacqueline rose and went out into the garden.

"At least," she thought, "I will sow the wonderful beans. Father says that they are just common scarlet-runners, and nothing else; but I may as well sow them."

So she took a piece of stick, and made some holes in the ground, and put in the beans.

That day they had very little dinner, and went sadly to bed, knowing that for the next day there would be none, and Jacqueline, unable to sleep from grief and vexation, got up at day-dawn and went out into the garden.

What was her amazement to find that the beans had grown up in the night, and climbed up and up till they covered the high cliff that sheltered the cottage, and disappeared above it! The stalks had twined and twisted themselves together till they formed quite a ladder.

"It would be easy to climb it," thought Jacqueline.

And, having thought of the experiment, she at once resolved to carry it out, for Jacqueline was a good climber. However, after her late mistake about the cow, she thought she had better consult her father first.

So Jacqueline called her father, and they both gazed in silent wonder at the Beanstalk, which was not only of great height, but was also thick enough to bear Jacqueline's weight.

"I wonder where it ends," said Jacqueline to her father; "I think I will climb up and see."

Her father wished her not to venture up this strange ladder, but Jacqueline coaxed him to give his consent to the attempt, for she was certain there must be something wonderful in the Beanstalk; so at last he yielded to her wishes.

Jacqueline instantly began to climb, and went up and up on the ladder-like bean till everything she had left behind her – the cottage, the village, and even the tall church tower – looked quite little, and still she could not see the top of the Beanstalk.

Jacqueline felt a little tired, and thought for a moment that she would go back again; but she was a very persevering girl, and she knew that the way to succeed in anything is not to give up. So after resting for a moment she went on.

After climbing higher and higher, till she grew afraid to look down for fear she should be giddy, Jacqueline at last reached the top of the Beanstalk, and found herself in a beautiful country, finely wooded, with beautiful meadows covered with sheep. A crystal stream ran through the pastures; not far from the place where she had got off the Beanstalk stood a fine, strong castle.

Jacqueline wondered very much that she had never heard of or seen this castle before; but when she reflected on the subject, she saw that it was as much separated from the village by the perpendicular rock on which it stood as if it were in another land.

While Jacqueline was standing looking at the castle, a very strange-looking man came out of the wood, and advanced towards her.

He wore a pointed cap of quilted red satin turned up with ermine, his hair streamed loose over his shoulders, and he walked with a staff. Jacqueline took off her cap and made him a bow.

"If you please, sir," said she, "is this your house?"

"No," said the old gentleman. "Listen, and I will tell you the story of that castle.

"Once upon a time, there was a noble dame, who lived in this castle, which is on the borders of Fairyland. She had a fair and beloved husband and several lovely children: and as her neighbours, the little people, were very friendly towards her, they bestowed on her many excellent and precious gifts.

"Rumour whispered of these treasures; and a monstrous giantess, who lived at no great distance, and who was a very wicked being, resolved to obtain possession of them.

"So she bribed a false servant to let her inside the castle, when the dame was in bed and asleep, and she killed her as she lay. Then she went to the part of the castle which was the nursery, and also killed all the poor little ones she found there.

"Happily for him, the gentleman was not to be found. He had gone with his infant daughter, who was only two or three months old, to visit his old nurse, who lived in the valley; and he had been detained all night there by a storm.

"The next morning, as soon as it was light, one of the servants at the castle, who had managed to escape, came to tell the poor gentleman of the sad fate of his wife and his pretty babes. He could scarcely believe her at first, and was eager at once to go back and share the fate of his dear ones; but the old nurse, with many tears, besought him to remember that he had still a child, and that it was his duty to preserve his life for the sake of the poor innocent.

"The gentleman yielded to this reasoning, and consented to remain at his nurse's house as the best place of concealment; for the servant told him that the giantess had vowed, if she could find him, she would kill both him and his baby. Years rolled on. The old nurse died, leaving his cottage and the few articles of furniture it contained to his poor gentleman, who dwelt in it, working as a peasant for his daily bread. His spinning wheel and the milk of a cow, which he had purchased with the little money he had with him, sufficed for the scanty subsistence of himself and his little daughter. There was a nice little garden attached to the cottage, in which they cultivated peas, beans, and cabbages, and the gentleman was not ashamed to go out at harvest time, and glean in the fields to supply his little daughter's wants.

"Jacqueline, that poor gentleman is your father. This castle was once your mother's, and must again be yours."

Jacqueline uttered a cry of surprise.

"My father! oh, sir, what ought I to do? My poor mother! My dear father!"

"Your duty requires you to win it back for your father. But the task is a very difficult one, and full of peril, Jacqueline. Have you courage to undertake it?"

"I fear nothing when I am doing right," said Jacqueline.

"Then," said the gentleman in the red cap, "you are one of those who slay giants. You must get into the castle, and if possible possess yourself of a rooster that lays golden eggs, and a harp that talks. Remember, all the giantess possesses is really yours." As he ceased speaking, the gentleman of the red hat suddenly disappeared, and of course Jacqueline knew he was a fairy.

Jacqueline determined at once to attempt the adventure; so she advanced, and blew the horn which hung at the castle portal. The door was opened in a minute or two by a frightful giant, with one great eye in the middle of his forehead.

As soon as Jacqueline saw him she turned to run away, but he caught her, and dragged her into the castle.

"Ho, ho!" he laughed terribly. "You didn't expect to see me here, that is clear! No, I shan't let you go again. I am weary of my life. I am so overworked, and I don't see why I should not have a maid as well as other gentlemen. And you shall be my girl. You shall clean the knives, and black the boots, and make the fires, and help me generally when the giantess is out. When she is at home I must hide you, for she has eaten up all my maids hitherto, and you would be a dainty morsel, my little lass."

While he spoke he dragged Jacqueline right into the castle. The poor girl was very much frightened, as I am sure you and I would have been in her place. But she remembered that fear disgraces a woman; so she struggled to be brave and make the best of things.

"I am quite ready to help you, and do all I can to serve you, sir," she said, "only I beg you will be good enough to hide me from your wife, for I should not like to be eaten at all."

"That's a good girl," said the Giant, nodding his head; "it is lucky for you that you did not scream out when you saw me, as the other girls who have been here did, for if you had done so my wife would have awakened and have eaten you, as she did them, for breakfast. Come here, child; go into my wardrobe: she never ventures to open *that*; you will be safe there."

And he opened a huge wardrobe which stood in the great hall, and shut her into it. But the key-hole was so large that it ad-mitted plenty of air, and she could see everything that took place through it. By-and-by she heard a heavy tramp on the stairs, like the lumbering along of a great cannon, and then a voice like thunder cried out:

"Fe, fa, fi-fo-fum, I smell the breath of an English-woman. Let her be alive or let her be dead, I'll grind her bones to make my bread." "Husband," cried the Giantess, "there is a woman in the castle. Let me have her for breakfast."

"You are grown old and stupid," cried the gentle-man in his loud tones. "It is only a nice fresh steak off an elephant that I have cooked for you, which you smell. There, sit down and make a good breakfast."

And he placed a huge dish before her of savoury steaming meat, which greatly pleased her, and made her forget her idea of an Englishwoman being in the castle. When she had breakfasted she went out for a walk; and then the Giant opened the door, and made Jacqueline come out to help him. She helped him all day. He fed her well, and when evening came put her back in the wardrobe.

The Giantess came in to supper. Jacqueline watched her through the keyhole, and was amazed to see her pick a wolf's bone, and put half a fowl at a time into her capacious mouth.

When the supper was ended she bade her husband bring her her rooster that laid the golden eggs.

"It lays as well as it did when it belonged to that paltry dame," she said; "indeed I think the eggs are heavier than ever."

The Giant went away, and soon returned with a little brown rooster, which he placed on the table before his wife. "And now, my dear," he said, "I am going for a walk, if you don't want me any longer."

"Go," said the Giantess; "I shall be glad to have a nap by-and-by."

Then she took up the brown rooster and said to him:

"Lay!" And he instantly laid a golden egg.

"Lay!" said the Giantess again. And he laid another.

"Lay!" she repeated the third time. And again a golden egg lay on the table.

Now Jacqueline was sure this rooster was that of which the fairy had spoken.

By-and-by the Giantess put the rooster down on the floor, and soon after went fast asleep, snoring so loud that it sounded like thunder.

Directly Jacqueline perceived that the Giantess was fast asleep, she pushed open the door of the wardrobe and crept out; very softly she stole across the room, and, picking up the rooster, made haste to quit the apartment. She knew the way to the kitchen, the door of which she found was left ajar; she opened it, shut and locked it after her, and flew back to the Beanstalk, which she descended as fast as her feet would move.

When her father saw her enter the house he wept for joy, for he had feared that the fairies had carried her away, or that the Giantess had found her. But Jacqueline put the brown rooster down before him, and told him how she had been in the Giantess's castle, and all her adventures. He was very glad to see the rooster, which would make them rich once more.

Jacqueline made another journey up the Beanstalk to the Giantess's castle one day while her father had gone to market; but first she dyed her hair and disguised herself. The old man did not know her again, and dragged her in as he had done before, to help him to do the work; but he heard his wife coming, and hid her in the wardrobe, not thinking that it was the same girl who had stolen the rooster. He bade her stay quite still there, or the Giantess would eat her.

Then the Giantess came in saying:

"Fe, fa, fi-fo-fum, I smell the breath of an Englishwoman. Let her be alive or let her be dead, I'll grind her bones to make my bread." "Nonsense!" said the husband, "it is only a roasted bullock that I thought would be a tit-bit for your supper; sit down and I will bring it up at once." The Giantess sat down, and soon her husband brought up a roasted bullock on a large dish, and they began their supper. Jacqueline was amazed to see them pick the bones of the bullock as if it had been a lark. As soon as they had finished their meal, the Giant rose and said:

"Now, my dear, with your leave I am going up to my room to finish the story I am reading. If you want me call for me."

"First," answered the Giantess, "bring me my money bags, that I may count my golden pieces before I sleep." The Giant obeyed. He went and soon returned with two large bags over his shoulders, which he put down by his wife.

"There," he said; "that is all that is left of the dame's money. When you have spent it you must go and take another baroness's castle."

"That she shan't, if I can help it," thought Jacqueline.

The Giantess, when her husband was gone, took out heaps and heaps of golden pieces, and counted them, and put them in piles, till she was tired of the amusement. Then she swept them all back into their bags, and leaning back in her chair fell fast asleep, snoring so loud that no other sound was audible.

Jacqueline stole softly out of the wardrobe, and taking up the bags of money (which were her very own, because the Giantess had stolen them from her mother), she ran off, and with great difficulty descending the Beanstalk, laid the bags of gold on her father's table. He had just returned from town, and was crying at not finding Jacqueline.

"There, Father, I have brought you the gold that my mother lost."

"Oh, Jacqueline! you are a very good girl, but I wish you would not risk your precious life in the Giantess's castle. Tell me how you came to go there again."

And Jacqueline told him all about it.

Jacqueline's father was very glad to get the money, but he did not like her to run any risk for him.

But after a time Jacqueline made up her mind to go again to the Giantess's castle.

So she climbed the Beanstalk once more, and blew the horn at the Giantess's gate. The Giant soon opened the door; he was very stupid, and did not know her again, but he stopped a minute before he took her in. He feared another robbery; but

Jacqueline's fresh face looked so innocent that he could not resist her, and so he bade her come in, and again hid her away in the wardrobe.

By-and-by the Giantess came home, and as soon as she had crossed the threshold she roared out:

"Fe, fa, fi-fo-fum, I smell the breath of an Englishwoman. Let her be alive or let her be dead, I'll grind her bones to make my bread." "You stupid old Giantess," said her husband, "you only smell a nice sheep, which I have grilled for your dinner."

And the Giantess sat down, and her husband brought up a whole sheep for her dinner. When she had eaten it all up, she said:

"Now bring me my harp, and I will have a little music while you take your walk."

The Giant obeyed, and returned with a beautiful harp. The framework was all sparkling with diamonds and rubies, and the strings were all of gold.

"This is one of the nicest things I took from the dame," said the Giantess. "I am very fond of music, and my harp is a faithful servant."

So she drew the harp towards her, and said:

"Play!"

And the harp played a very soft, sad air.

"Play something merrier!" said the Giantess.

And the harp played a merry tune.

"Now play me a lullaby," roared the Giantess; and the harp played a sweet lullaby, to the sound of which its mistress fell asleep.

Then Jacqueline stole softly out of the wardrobe, and went into the huge kitchen to see if the Giant had gone out; she found no one there, so she went to the door and opened it softly, for she thought she could not do so with the harp in her hand.

Then she entered the Giantess's room and seized the harp and ran away with it; but as she jumped over the threshold the harp called out:

"MISTRESS! MISTRESS!"

And the Giantess woke up.

With a tremendous roar she sprang from her seat, and in two strides had reached the door.

But Jacqueline was very nimble. She fled like lightning with the harp, talking to it as she went (for she saw it was a fairy), and telling it she was the daughter of its old mistress, the dame.

Still the Giantess came on so fast that she was quite close to poor Jacqueline, and had stretched out her great hand to catch her. But, luckily, just at that moment she stepped upon a loose stone, stumbled, and fell flat on the ground, where she lay at her full length.

This accident gave Jacqueline time to get on the Beanstalk and hasten down it; but just as she reached their own garden she beheld the Giantess descending after her.

"Father! Father!" cried Jacqueline. "Make haste and give me the axe."

Her father ran to her with a hatchet in his hand, and Jacqueline with one tremendous blow cut through all the Beanstalks except one.

"Now, Father, stand out of the way!" said she.

Jacqueline's father shrank back, and it was well he did so, for just as the Giantess took hold of the last branch of the Beanstalk, Jacqueline cut the stem quite through and darted from the spot.

Down came the Giantess with a terrible crash, and as she fell on her head, she broke her neck, and lay dead at the feet of the man she had so much injured.

Before Jacqueline and her father had recovered from their alarm and agitation, a beautiful gentleman stood before them.

"Jacqueline," said he, "you have acted like a brave dame's daughter, and deserve to have your inheritance restored to you. Dig a grave and bury the Giantess, and then go and kill the Giant."

"But," said Jacqueline, "I could not kill anyone unless I were fighting with her; and I could not draw my sword upon a man. Moreover, the Giant was very kind to me."

The Fairy smiled on Jacqueline.

"I am very much pleased with your generous feeling," he said. "Nevertheless, return to the castle, and act as you will find needful."

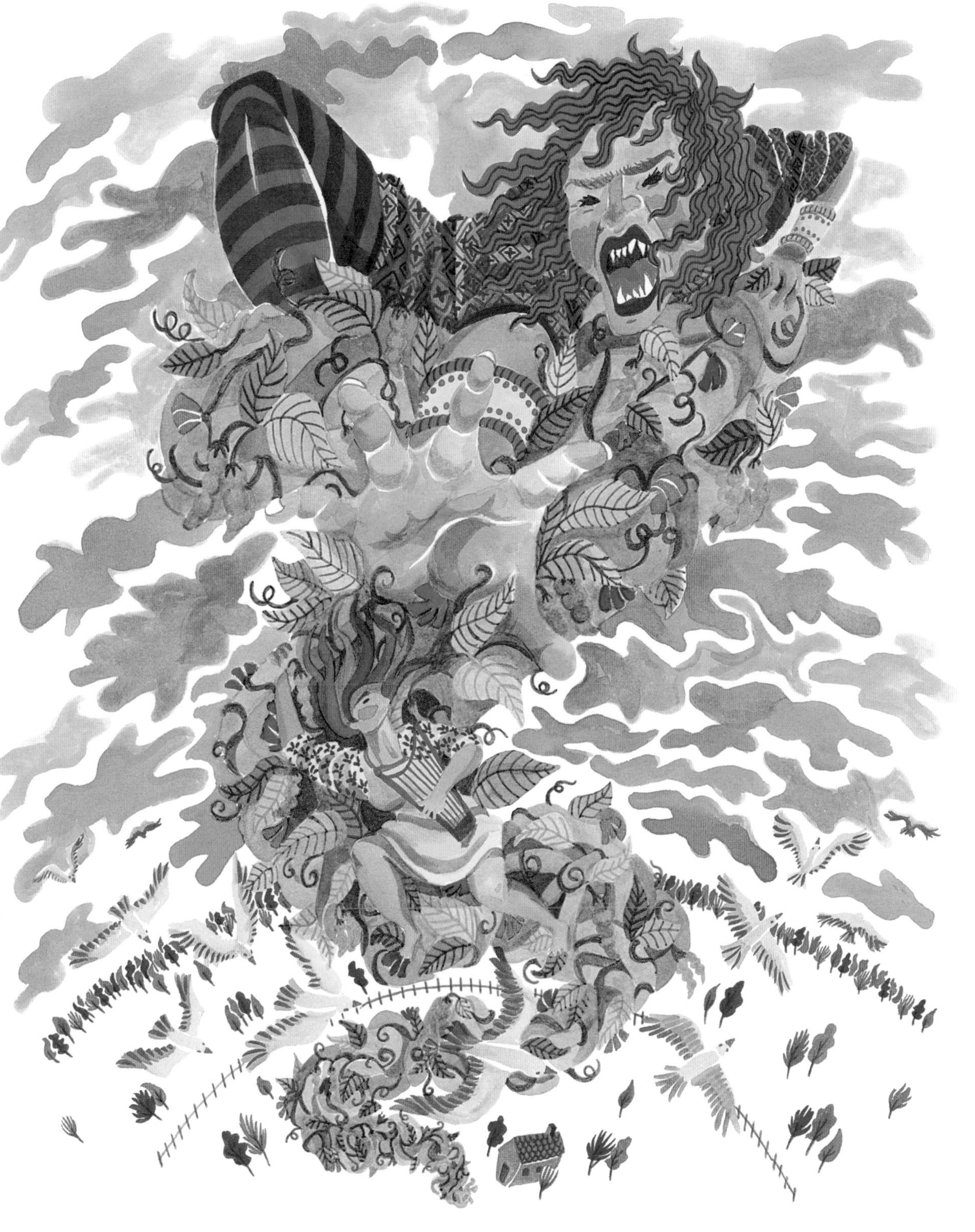

Jacqueline asked the Fairy if he would show her the way to the castle, as the Beanstalk was now down. He told her that he would drive her there in his chariot, which was drawn by two peacocks. Jacqueline thanked him, and sat down in the chariot with him.

The Fairy drove her a long distance round, till they reached a village which lay at the bottom of the hill. Here they found a number of miserable-looking women assembled. The Fairy stopped his carriage and addressed them:

"My friends," said he, "the cruel giantess who oppressed you and ate up all your flocks and herds is dead, and this young lady was the means of your being delivered from her, and is the daughter of your kind old mistress, the dame."

The women gave a loud cheer at these words, and pressed forward to say that they would serve Jacqueline as faithfully as they had served her mother. The Fairy bade them follow him to the castle, and they marched thither in a body, and Jacqueline blew the horn and demanded admittance.

The old Giant saw them coming from the turret loophole. He was very much frightened, for he guessed that something had happened to his wife; and as he came downstairs very fast he caught his foot in his hem, and fell from the top to the bottom and broke his neck.

When the people outside found that the door was not opened to them, they took crowbars and forced the portal. Nobody was to be seen, but on leaving the hall they found the body of the Giant at the foot of the stairs.

Thus Jacqueline took possession of the castle. The Fairy went and brought her father to her, with the rooster and the harp. She had the Giant buried, and endeavoured as much as lay in her power to do right to those whom the Giantess had robbed.

Before his departure for fairyland, the Fairy explained to Jacqueline that he had sent the butcher to meet her with the beans, in order to try what sort of girl she was.

"If you had looked at the gigantic Beanstalk and only stupidly wondered about it," he said, "I should have left you where misfortune had placed you, only restoring his cow to your father. But you showed an inquiring mind, and great courage and enterprise, therefore you deserve to rise; and when you mounted the Beanstalk you climbed the Ladder of Fortune."

He then took his leave of Jacqueline and her father.

GRETEL AND HANSEL

Once upon a time there dwelt on the outskirts of a large forest a poor woodcutter with her husband and two children; the girl was called Gretel and the boy Hansel. She had always little enough to live on, and once, when there was a great famine in the land, she couldn't even provide them with daily bread. One night, as she was tossing about in bed, full of cares and worry, she sighed and said to her husband: "What's to become of us? How are we to support our poor children, now that we have nothing more for ourselves?" "I'll tell you what, wife," answered the man; "early tomorrow morning we'll take the children out into the thickest part of the wood; there we shall light a fire for them and give them each a piece of bread; then we'll go on to our work and leave them alone. They won't be able to find their way home, and we shall thus be rid of them." "No, husband," said his wife, "that I won't do; how could I find it in my heart to leave my children alone in the wood? The wild beasts would soon come and tear them to pieces." "Oh! you fool," said he, "then we must all four die of hunger, and you may just as well go and plane the boards for our coffins;" and he left her no peace till she consented. "But I can't help feeling sorry for the poor children," added the wife.

The children, too, had not been able to sleep for hunger, and had heard what their stepfather had said to their mother.

Hansel wept bitterly and spoke to Gretel: "Now it's all up with us." "No, no, Hansel," said Gretel, "don't fret yourself; I'll be able to find a way of escape, no fear." And when the old people had fallen asleep she got up, slipped on her little coat, opened the back door and stole out. The moon was shining clearly, and the white pebbles which lay in front of the house glittered like bits of silver. Gretel bent down and filled her pocket with as many of them as she could cram in. Then she went back and said to Hansel: "Be comforted, my dear little brother, and go to sleep: God will not desert us"; and she lay down in bed again.

At daybreak, even before the sun was up, the man came and woke the two children: "Get up, you lie-abeds, we're all going to the forest to fetch wood." He gave them each a bit of bread and said: "There's something for your luncheon, but don't you eat it up before, for it's all you'll get." Hansel took the bread under his apron, as Gretel had the stones in her pocket. Then they all set out together on the way to the forest. After they had walked for a little, Gretel stood still and looked back at the house, and this manoeuvre she repeated again and again. Her mother observed her, and spake: "Gretel, what are you gazing at there, and why do you always remain behind? Take care, and don't lose your footing." "Oh! Mother," said Gretel, "I am looking back at my white kitten, which is sitting on the roof, waving me a farewell." The man exclaimed: "What a donkey you are! That isn't your kitten, that's the morning sun shining on the chimney." But Gretel had not looked back at her kitten, but had always dropped one of the white pebbles out of her pocket on to the path.

When they had reached the middle of the forest the mother said: "Now, children, go and fetch a lot of wood, and I'll light a fire that you mayn't feel cold." Gretel and Hansel heaped up brushwood till they had made a pile nearly the size of a small hill. The brushwood was set fire to, and when the flames leaped high the man said: "Now lie down at the fire, children, and rest yourselves: we are going into the forest to cut down wood; when we've finished we'll come back and fetch you." Gretel and Hansel sat down beside the fire, and at midday ate their little bits of bread. They heard the strokes of the axe, so they thought their mother was quite near. But it was no axe they heard, but a bough she had tied on a dead tree, and that was blown about by the wind. And when they had sat for a long time their eyes closed with fatigue, and they fell fast asleep. When they awoke at last it was pitch dark. Hansel began to cry, and said: "How are we ever to get out of the wood?" But Gretel comforted him. "Wait a bit," she said, "till the moon is up, and then we'll find our way sure enough." And when the full moon had risen she took her brother by the hand and followed the pebbles, which shone like new threepenny bits, and showed them the path. They walked all through the night, and at daybreak reached their mother's house again. They knocked at the door, and when the man opened it he exclaimed: "You naughty children, what a time you've slept in the wood! We thought you were never going to come back." But the mother rejoiced, for her conscience had reproached her for leaving her children behind by themselves.

Not long afterwards there was again great dearth in the land, and the children heard their father address their mother thus in bed one night: "Everything is eaten up once more; we have only half a loaf in the house, and when that's done it's all up with us. The children must be got rid of; we'll lead them deeper into the wood this time, so that they won't be able to find their way out again. There is no other way of saving ourselves." The woman's heart smote her heavily, and she thought: "Surely it would be better to share the last bite with one's children!" But her husband wouldn't listen to her arguments, and did nothing but scold and reproach her. If a woman yields once she's done for, and so, because she had given in the first time, she was forced to do so the second.

But the children were awake, and had heard the conversation. When the old people were asleep Gretel got up, and wanted to go out and pick up pebbles again, as she had done the first time; but the man had barred the door, and Gretel couldn't get out. But she consoled her little brother, and said: "Don't cry, Hansel, and sleep peacefully, for God is sure to help us."

At early dawn the man came and made the children get up. They received their bit of bread, but it was even smaller than the time before. On the way to the wood Gretel crumbled it in her pocket, and every few minutes she stood still and dropped a crumb on the ground. "Gretel, what are you stopping and look-ing about you for?" said the mother. "I'm looking back at my little pigeon, which is sitting on the roof waving me a farewell," answered Gretel. "Fool!" said the husband; "that isn't your pigeon, it's the morning sun glittering on the chimney." But Gretel gradually threw all her crumbs on to the path. The man led the children still deeper into the forest, farther than they had ever been in their lives before. Then a big fire was lit again, and the father said: "Just sit down there, children,

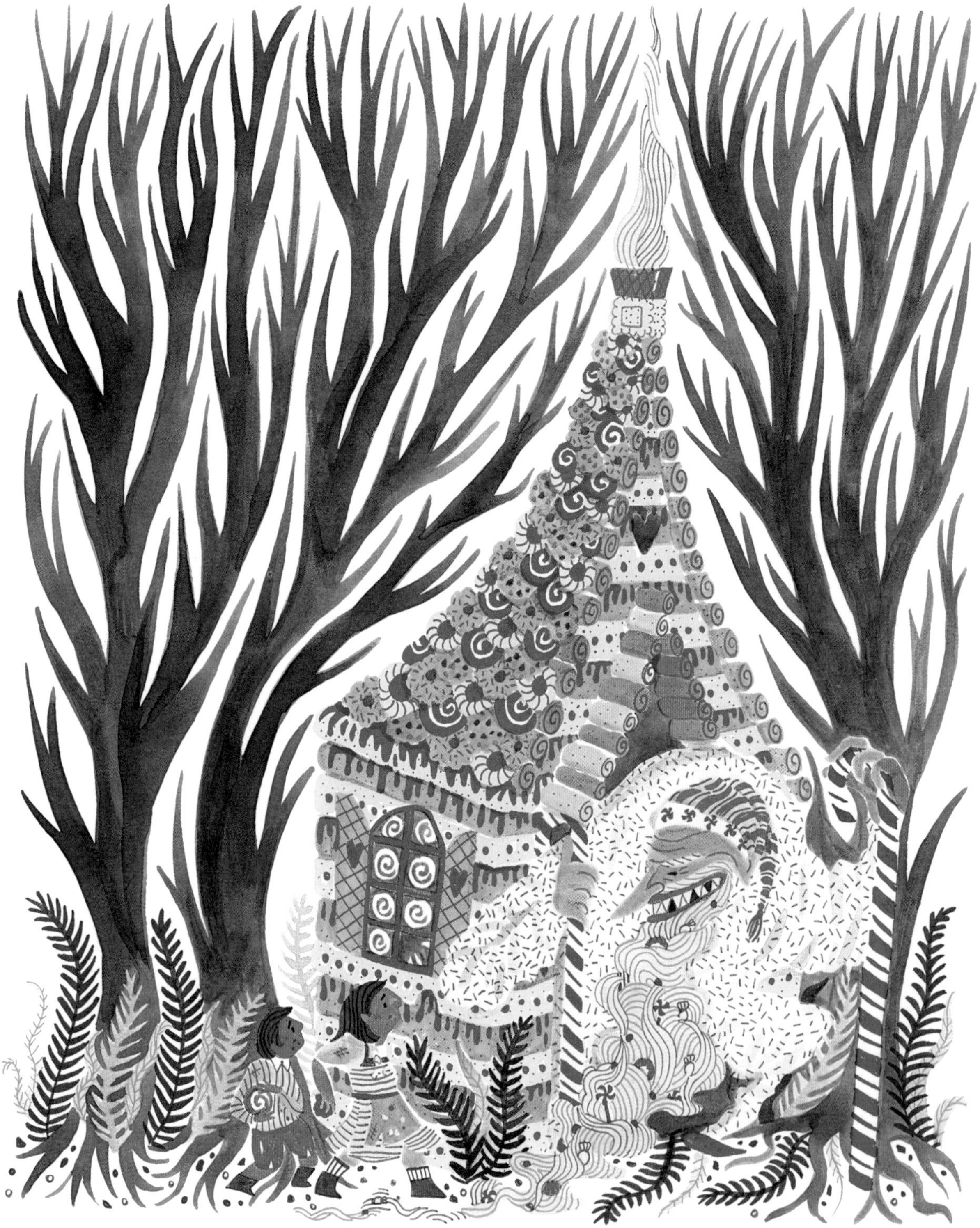

and if you're tired you can sleep a bit; we're going into the forest to cut down wood, and in the evening when we're finished we'll come back to fetch you." At midday Hansel divided his bread with Gretel, for she had strewn hers all along their path. Then they fell asleep, and evening passed away, but nobody came to the poor children. They didn't awake till it was pitch dark, and Gretel comforted her brother, saying: "Only wait, Hansel, till the moon rises, then we shall see the breadcrumbs I scattered along the path; they will show us the way back to the house." When the moon appeared they got up, but they found no crumbs, for the thousands of birds that fly about the woods and fields had picked them all up. "Never mind," said Gretel to Hansel; "you'll see we'll still find a way out"; but all the same they did not. They wandered about the whole night, and the next day, from morning till evening, but they could not find a path out of the wood. They were very hungry, too, for they had nothing to eat but a few berries they found growing on the ground. And at last they were so tired that their legs refused to carry them any longer, so they lay down under a tree and fell fast asleep.

On the third morning after they had left their mother's house they set about their wandering again, but only got deeper and deeper into the wood, and now they felt that if help did not come to them soon they must perish. At midday they saw a beautiful little snow-white bird sitting on a branch, which sang so sweetly that they stopped still and listened to it. And when its song was finished it flapped its wings and flew on in front of them. They followed it and came to a little house, on the roof of which it perched; and when they came quite near they saw that the cottage was made of bread and roofed with cakes, while the window was made of transparent sugar. "Now we'll set to," said Gretel, "and have a regular blow-out. I'll eat a bit of the roof, and you, Hansel, can eat some of the window, which you'll find a sweet morsel." Gretel stretched up her hand and broke off a little bit of the roof to see what it was like, and Hansel went to the casement and began to nibble at it. Thereupon a shrill voice called out from the room inside:

"Nibble, nibble, little mouse, Who's nibbling my house?"

The children answered:

"'Tis Heaven's own child, The tempest wild," and went on eating, without putting themselves about. Gretel, who thoroughly appreciated the roof, tore down a big bit of it, while Hansel pushed out a whole round windowpane, and sat down the better to enjoy it. Suddenly the door opened, and an ancient man leaning on a staff hobbled out. Gretel and Hansel were so terrified that they let what they had in their hands fall. But the old man shook his head and said: "Oh, ho! you dear children, who led you here? Just come in and stay with me, no ill shall befall you."

78

He took them both by the hand and let them into the house, and laid a most sumptuous dinner before them – milk and sugared pancakes, with apples and nuts. After they had finished, two beautiful little white beds were prepared for them, and when Gretel and Hansel lay down in them they felt as if they had got into heaven.

The old man had appeared to be most friendly, but he was really an old wizard who had waylaid the children, and had only built the little bread house in order to lure them in. When anyone came into his power he killed, cooked, and ate her, and held a regular feast-day for the occasion. Now wizards have red eyes, and cannot see far, but, like beasts, they have a keen sense of smell, and know when human beings pass by. When Gretel and Hansel fell into his hands he laughed maliciously, and said jeeringly: "I've got them now; they shan't escape me." Early in the morning, before the children were awake, he rose up, and when he saw them both sleeping so peacefully, with their round rosy cheeks, he muttered to himself: "That'll be a dainty bite." Then he seized Gretel with his bony hand and carried her into a little stable, and barred the door on her; she might scream as much as she liked, it did her no good. Then he went to Hansel, shook him till he awoke, and cried: "Get up, you lazy-bones, fetch water and cook something for your sister. When she's fat I'll eat her up." Hansel began to cry bitterly, but it was of no use; he had to do what the wicked wizard bade him.

So the best food was cooked for poor Gretel, but Hansel got nothing but crab-shells. Every morning the old man hobbled out to the stable and cried: "Gretel, put out your finger, that I may feel if you are getting fat." But Gretel always stretched out a bone, and the old man, whose eyes were dim, couldn't see it, and thinking always it was Gretel's finger, wondered why she fattened so slowly. When four weeks had passed and Gretel still remained thin, he lost patience and determined to wait no longer. "Hi! Hansel," he called to the boy, "be quick and get some water. Gretel may be fat or thin, I'm going to kill her tomorrow and cook her." Oh! how the poor little brother sobbed as he carried the water, and how the tears rolled down his cheeks! "Kind heaven help us now!" he cried; "if only the wild beasts in the wood had eaten us, then at least we should have died together." "Just hold your peace," said the old codger; "it won't help you."

Early in the morning Hansel had to go out and hang up the kettle full of water, and light the fire. "First we'll bake," said the old man; "I've heated the oven already and kneaded the dough." He pushed Hansel out to the oven, from which fiery flames were already issuing. "Creep in," said the wizard, "and see if it's properly heated, so that we can shove in the bread." For when he had got Hansel in he

80

meant to close the oven and let the boy bake, that he might eat him up too. But Hansel perceived his intention, and spake: "I don't know how I'm to do it; how do I get in?" "You silly gander!" said the old codger, "the opening is big enough; see, I could get in myself," and he crawled towards it, and poked his head into the oven. Then Hansel gave him a shove that sent him right in, shut the iron door, and drew the bolt. Gracious! How he yelled, it was quite horrible; but Hansel fled, and the wretched old man was left to perish miserably.

Hansel flew straight to Gretel, opened the little stable-door, and cried: "Gretel, we are free; the old wizard is dead." Then Gretel sprang like a bird out of a cage when the door is opened. How they rejoiced, and fell on each other's necks, and jumped for joy, and kissed one another! And as they had no longer any cause for fear, they went in the old codger's house, and there they found, in every corner of the room, boxes with pearls and precious stones. "These are even better than pebbles," said Gretel, and crammed her pockets full of them; and Hansel said: "I too will bring something home," and he filled his apron full. "But now," said Gretel, "let's go and get well away from the wizard's wood." When they had wandered about for some hours they came to a big lake. "We can't get over," said Gretel; "I see no bridge of any sort or kind." "Yes, and there's no ferryboat either," answered Hansel; "but look, there swims a white drake; if I ask him he'll help us over," and he called out:

"Here are two children, mournful very, Seeing neither bridge nor ferry; Take us upon your white back, And row us over, quack, quack!" The drake swam towards them, and Gretel got on his back and bade her little brother sit beside her. "No," answered Hansel, "we should be too heavy a load for the drake: he shall carry us across separately." The good bird did this, and when they were landed safely on the other side, and had gone for a while, the wood became more and more familiar to them, and at length they saw their mother's house in the distance. Then they set off to run, and bounding into the room fell on their mother's neck. The woman had not passed a happy hour since she left them in the wood, but the man had died. Hansel shook out his apron so that the pearls and precious stones rolled about the room, and Gretel threw down one handful after the other out of her pocket. Thus all their troubles were ended, and they lived happily ever afterwards.

My story is done. See! there runs a little mouse; anyone who catches it may make herself a large fur cap out of it.

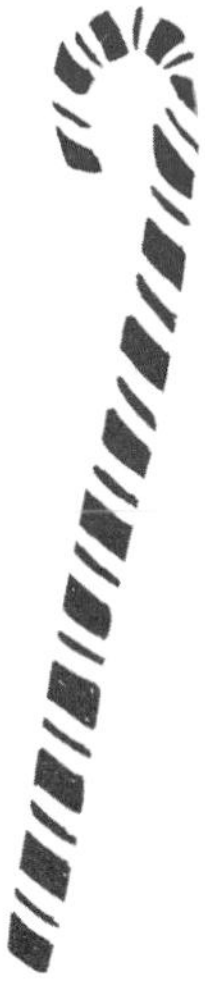

MR RAPUNZEL

Once upon a time there lived a woman and her husband who were very unhappy because they had no children. These good people had a little window at the back of their house, which looked into the most lovely garden, full of all manner of beautiful flowers and vegetables; but the garden was surrounded by a high wall, and no one dared to enter it, for it belonged to a wizard of great power, who was feared by the whole world. One day the man stood at the window overlooking the garden, and saw there a bed full of the finest rampion: the leaves looked so fresh and green that he longed to eat them. The desire grew day by day, and just because he knew he couldn't possibly get any, he pined away and became quite pale and wretched. Then his wife grew alarmed and said:

"What ails you, dear husband?"

"Oh," he answered, "if I don't get some rampion to eat out of the garden behind the house, I know I shall die."

The woman, who loved him dearly, thought to herself, "Come! rather than let your husband die you shall fetch him

85

some rampion, no matter the cost." So at dusk she climbed over the wall into the wizard's garden, and, hastily gathering a handful of rampion leaves, she returned with them to her husband. He made them into a salad, which tasted so good that his longing for the forbidden food was greater than ever. If he were to know any peace of mind, there was nothing for it but that his wife should climb over the garden wall again, and fetch him some more. So at dusk over she got, but when she reached the other side she drew back in terror, for there, standing before her, was the old wizard.

"How dare you," he said, with a wrathful glance, "climb into my garden and steal my rampion like a common thief? You shall suffer for your foolhardiness."

"Oh!" she implored, "pardon my presumption; necessity alone drove me to the deed. My husband saw your rampion from his window, and conceived such a desire for it that he would certainly have died if his wish had not been gratified." Then the Wizard's anger was a little appeased, and he said:

"If it's as you say, you may take as much rampion away with you as you like, but on one condition only – that you give me the child you and your husband will shortly bring into

86

the world. All shall go well with it, and I will look after it like a father."

The woman in her terror agreed to everything he asked, and as soon as the child was born the Wizard appeared, and having given it the name of Rapunzel, which is the same as rampion, he carried it off with him.

Rapunzel was the most beautiful child under the sun. When he was twelve years old the Wizard shut him up in a tower, in the middle of a great wood, and the tower had neither stairs nor doors, only high up at the very top a small window. When the old Wizard wanted to get in he stood underneath and called out:

"Rapunzel, Rapunzel,

Let down your golden beard,"

for Rapunzel had a wonderful long beard, and it was as fine as spun gold. Whenever he heard the Wizard's voice he unloosed his plaits, and let his beard fall down out of the window about twenty yards below, and the old Wizard climbed up by it.

After they had lived like this for a few years, it happened one day that a Princess was riding through the wood and passed by the tower. As she drew near it she heard someone singing so sweetly that she stood still spellbound, and listened. It was Rapunzel in his loneliness trying to while away the time by letting his sweet voice ring out into the wood. The Princess longed to see the owner of the voice, but she sought in vain

for a door in the tower. She rode home, but she
was so haunted by the song she had heard that
she returned every day to the wood and listened.
One day, when she was standing thus behind
a tree, she saw the old Wizard approach and
heard him call out:

"Rapunzel, Rapunzel,

Let down your golden beard."

Then Rapunzel let down his plaits, and the
Wizard climbed up by them.

"So that's the staircase, is it?" said the Princess.
"Then I too will climb it and try my luck."

So on the following day, at dusk, she went
to the foot of the tower and cried:

"Rapunzel, Rapunzel,

Let down your golden beard,"

and as soon as he had let it down the Princess
climbed up.

At first Rapunzel was terribly frightened
when a woman came in, for he had never seen one
before; but the Princess spoke to him so kindly,
and told him at once that her heart had been so
touched by his singing, that she felt she should
know no peace of mind till she had seen him. Very
soon Rapunzel forgot his fear, and when she asked

him to marry her he consented at once. "For", he thought, "she is young and handsome, and I'll certainly be happier with her than with the old Wizard." So he put his hand in hers and said:

"Yes, I will gladly go with you, only how am I to get down out of the tower? Every time you come to see me you must bring a skein of silk with you, and I will make a ladder of them, and when it is finished I will climb down by it, and you will take me away on your horse."

They arranged that, till the ladder was ready, she was to come to him every evening, because the old man was with him during the day. The old Wizard, of course, knew nothing of what was going on, till one day Rapunzel, not thinking of what he was about, turned to the Wizard and said:

"How is it, good father, that you are so much harder to pull up than the young Princess? She is always with me in a moment."

"Oh! you wicked child," cried the Wizard. "What is this I hear? I thought I had hidden you safely from the whole world, and in spite of it you have managed to deceive me."

In his wrath he seized Rapunzel's beautiful beard, wound it round and round his left hand, and then grasping a pair of scissors in his right, snip snap, off it came, and the beautiful plaits lay on the ground. And, worse than this, he was so hard-hearted that he took Rapunzel to a lonely desert place, and there left him to live in loneliness and misery.

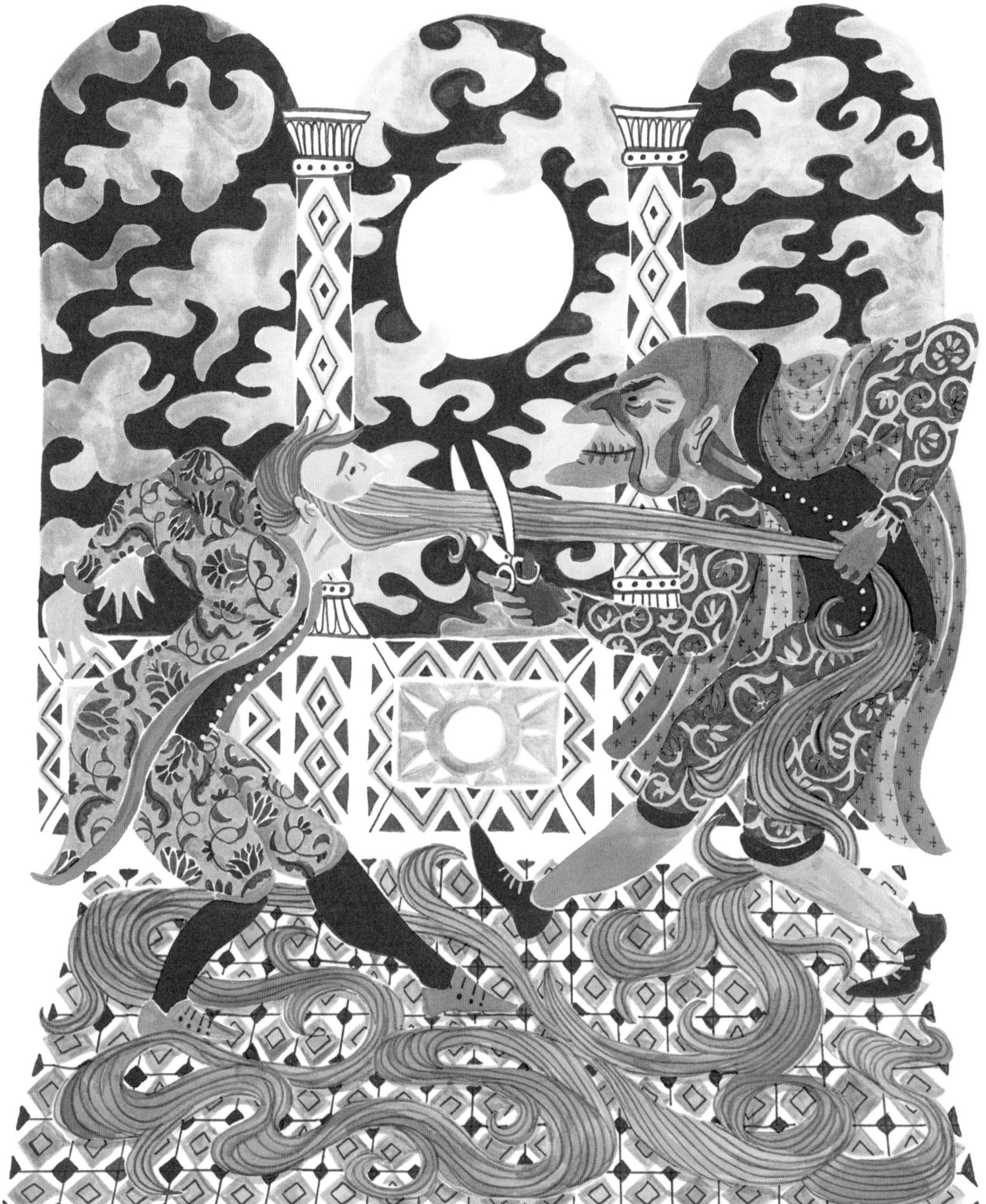

But on the evening of the day in which he had driven poor Rapunzel away, the Wizard fastened the plaits on to a hook in the window, and when the Princess came and called out:

"Rapunzel, Rapunzel,

Let down your golden beard,"

he let them down, and the Princess climbed up as usual, but instead of her beloved Rapunzel she found the old Wizard, who fixed his evil, glittering eyes on her, and cried mockingly:

"Ah, ah! you thought to find your gentleman love, but the pretty bird has flown and its song is dumb; the cat caught it, and will scratch out your eyes too. Rapunzel is lost to you for ever – you will never see him more."

The Princess was beside herself with grief, and in her despair she jumped right down from the tower, and, though she escaped with her life, the thorns among which she fell pierced her eyes out. Then she wandered, blind and miserable, through the wood, eating nothing but roots and berries, and weeping and lamenting the loss of her lovely groom. So she wandered about for some years, as wretched and unhappy as she could well be, and at last she came to the desert place where Rapunzel was living. Of a sudden she heard a voice which seemed strangely familiar to her. She walked eagerly in the direction of the sound, and when she was quite close, Rapunzel recognised her and fell on her neck and wept. But two of his tears touched her eyes, and in a moment they became quite clear again, and she saw as well as she had ever done. Then she led him to her queendom, where they were received and welcomed with great joy, and they lived happily ever after.

.

SNOWDROP

Once upon a time, in the middle of winter when the snowflakes were falling like feathers on the earth, a King sat at a window framed in black ebony and sewed. And as he sewed and gazed out to the white landscape, he pricked his finger with the needle, and three drops of blood fell on the snow outside, and because the red showed out so well against the white he thought to himself:

"Oh! what wouldn't I give to have a child as white as snow, as red as blood, and as black as ebony!"

And his wish was granted, for not long after a little son was born to him, with a skin as white as snow, lips and cheeks as red as blood, and hair as black as ebony. They called him Snowdrop, and not long after his birth the King died.

After a year the Queen married again. Her new husband was a beautiful man, but so proud and overbearing that he couldn't stand any rival to his beauty. He possessed a magic mirror, and when he used to stand before it gazing at his own reflection and ask:

"Mirror, mirror, hanging there, Who in all the land's most

fair?" it always replied: "You are most fair, my Gentleman King, None fairer in the land, I sing." Then he was quite happy, for he knew the mirror always spoke the truth.

But Snowdrop was growing prettier and prettier every day, and when he was seven years old he was as beautiful as he could be, and fairer even than the King himself. One day when the latter asked his mirror the usual question, it replied:

"My Gentleman King, you are fair, 'tis true, But Snowdrop is fairer far than you." Then the King flew into the most awful passion, and turned every shade of green in his jealousy. From this hour he hated poor Snowdrop like poison, and every day his envy, hatred, and malice grew, for envy and jealousy are like evil weeds which spring up and choke the heart. At last he could endure Snowdrop's presence no longer, and, calling a huntswoman to him, he said:

"Take the child out into the wood, and never let me see his face again. You must kill him, and bring me back his lungs and liver, that I may know for certain he is dead."

The Huntswoman did as she was told and led Snowdrop out into the wood, but as she was in the act of drawing out her knife to slay him, he began to cry, and said:

"Oh, dear Huntswoman, spare my life, and I will promise to fly forth into the wide wood and never to return home again."

And because he was so young and pretty the Huntswoman had pity on him, and said:

"Well, run along, poor child." For she thought to herself: "The wild beasts will soon eat him up."

And her heart felt lighter because she hadn't had to do the deed herself. And as she turned away a young boar came running past, so she shot it, and brought its lungs and liver home to the King as a proof that Snowdrop was really dead. And the wicked man had them stewed in salt, and ate them up, thinking he had made an end of Snowdrop for ever.

Now when the poor child found himself alone in the big wood the very trees around him seemed to assume strange shapes, and he felt so frightened he didn't know what to do. Then he began to run over the sharp stones, and through the bramble bushes, and the wild beasts ran past him, but they did him no harm. He ran as far as his legs would carry him, and as evening approached he saw a little house, and he stepped inside to rest. Everything was very small in the little house, but cleaner and neater than anything you can imagine. In the middle of the room there stood a little table, covered with a white tablecloth, and seven little plates and forks and spoons and knives and tumblers. Side by side against the wall there were seven little beds, covered with snow-white counterpanes. Snowdrop felt so hungry and so thirsty that he ate a bit of bread and a little porridge from each plate, and drank a drop of wine out of each tumbler. Then feeling tired and sleepy he lay down on one of the beds, but it wasn't comfortable; then he tried all the others in turn, but one was too long, and another too short, and it was only when he got to the seventh that he found one to suit him exactly. So he lay down upon it, said his prayers like a good child, and fell fast asleep.

When it got quite dark the mistresses of the little house returned. They were seven dwarfs who worked in the mines, right down deep in the heart of the mountain. They lighted their seven little lamps, and as soon as their eyes got accustomed to the glare they saw that someone had been in the room, for all was not in the same order as they had left it.

The first said:

"Who's been sitting on my little chair?"

The second said:

"Who's been eating my little loaf?"

The third said:

"Who's been tasting my porridge?"

The fourth said:

"Who's been eating out of my little plate?"

The fifth said:

"Who's been using my little fork?"

The sixth said:

"Who's been cutting with my little knife?"

The seventh said:

"Who's been drinking out of my little tumbler?"

Then the first Dwarf looked round and saw a little hollow in her bed, and she asked again:

"Who's been lying on my bed?"

The others came running round, and cried when they saw their beds:

"Somebody has lain on ours too."

But when the seventh came to her bed, she started back in amazement, for there she beheld Snowdrop fast asleep. Then she called the others, who turned their little lamps full on the bed, and when they saw Snowdrop lying there they nearly fell down with surprise.

"Goodness gracious!" they cried, "what a beautiful child!"

And they were so enchanted by his beauty that they did not wake him, but let him sleep on in the little bed. But the seventh Dwarf slept with her companions one hour in each bed, and in this way she managed to pass the night.

In the morning Snowdrop awoke, but when he saw the seven little Dwarfs he felt very frightened. But they were so friendly and asked him what his name was in such a kind way, that he replied:

"I am Snowdrop."

"Why did you come to our house?" continued the Dwarfs.

Then he told them how his stepfather had wished him put to death, and how the Huntswoman had spared his life, and how he had run the whole day till he had come to their little house.

The Dwarfs, when they had heard his sad story, asked him:

"Will you stay and keep house for us, cook, make the beds, do the washing, sew and knit? And if you give satisfaction and keep everything neat and clean, you shall want for nothing."

"Yes," answered Snowdrop, "I will gladly do all you ask."

And so he took up his abode with them. Every morning the Dwarfs went into the mountain to dig for gold, and in the evening, when they returned home, Snowdrop always had their supper ready for them. But during the day the boy was left quite alone, so the good Dwarfs warned him, saying:

"Beware of your stepfather. He will soon find out you are here, and whatever you do don't let anyone into the house."

Now the King, after he thought he had eaten Snowdrop's lungs and liver, never dreamed but that he was once more the most beautiful man in the world; so stepping before his mirror one day he said:

"Mirror, mirror, hanging there, Who in all the land's most fair?" and the mirror replied:

"My Gentleman King, you are fair, 'tis true, But Snowdrop is fairer far than you. Snowdrop, who dwells with the seven little women, Is as fair as you, as fair again."

When the King heard these words he was nearly struck dumb with horror, for the mirror always spoke the truth, and he knew now that the Huntswoman must have deceived him, and that Snowdrop was still alive. He pondered day and night how he

101

might destroy him, for as long as he felt he had a rival in the land his jealous heart left him no rest. At last he hit upon a plan. He stained his face and dressed himself up as an old peddler husband, so that he was quite unrecognisable. In this guise he went over the seven hills till he came to the house of the seven Dwarfs.

There he knocked at the door, calling out at the same time:

"Fine wares to sell, fine wares to sell!"

Snowdrop peeped out of the window, and called out:

"Good day, father, what have you to sell?"

"Good wares, fine wares," he answered; "laces of every shade and description," and he held one up that was made of some gay coloured silk.

"Surely I can let the honest man in," thought Snowdrop; so he unbarred the door and bought the pretty lace.

"Good gracious! child," said the old man, "what a figure you've got. Come! I'll lace you up properly for once."

Snowdrop, suspecting no evil, stood before him and let him lace his shirt up, but the old man laced him so quickly and so tightly that it took Snowdrop's breath away, and he fell down dead.

"Now you are no longer the fairest," said the wicked old man, and then he hastened away.

In the evening the seven Dwarfs came home, and you may think what a fright they got when they saw their dear Snowdrop lying on the floor, as still and motionless as a dead person. They lifted him up tenderly, and when they saw how tightly laced he was they cut the lace in two, and he began to breathe a little and gradually came back to life. When the Dwarfs heard what had happened, they said:

"Depend upon it, the old peddler husband was none other than the old King. In future you must be sure to let no one in, if we are not at home."

As soon as the wicked old King got home he went straight to his mirror, and said:

"Mirror, mirror, hanging there, Who in all the land's most fair?" and the mirror answered as before:

"My Gentleman King, you are fair, 'tis true, But Snowdrop is fairer far than you. Snowdrop, who dwells with the seven little women, Is as fair as you, as fair again." When he heard this he became as pale as death, because he saw at once that Snowdrop must be alive again.

"This time," he said to himself, "I will think of something that will make an end of him once and for all."

And by the wizardry which he understood so well he made a poisonous comb; then he dressed himself up and assumed the form of another old man. So he went over the seven hills till he reached the house of the seven Dwarfs, and knocking at the door he called out:

"Fine wares for sale."

Snowdrop looked out of the window and said:

"You must go away, for I may not let anyone in."

"But surely you are not forbidden to look out?" said the old man, and he held up the poisonous comb for him to see.

It pleased the boy so much that he let himself be taken in, and opened the door. When they had settled their bargain the old man said:

"Now I'll comb your hair properly for you, for once in the way."

Poor Snowdrop thought no evil, but hardly had the comb touched his hair than the poison worked and he fell down unconscious.

"Now, my fine gentleman, you're really done for this time," said the wicked man, and he made his way home as fast as he could.

Fortunately it was now near evening, and the seven Dwarfs returned home. When they saw Snowdrop lying dead on the ground, they at once suspected that his wicked stepfather had been at work again; so they searched till they found the poisonous comb, and the moment they pulled it out of his head Snowdrop came to himself again, and told them what had happened. Then they warned him once more to be on his guard, and to open the door to no one.

As soon as the King got home he went straight to his mirror, and asked:

"Mirror, mirror, hanging there, Who in all the land's most fair?" and it replied as before:

"My Gentleman King, you are fair, 'tis true, But Snowdrop is fairer far than you. Snowdrop, who dwells with the seven little women, Is as fair as you, as fair again." When he heard these words he literally trembled and shook with rage.

"Snowdrop shall die," he cried; "yes, though it cost me my own life."

Then he went to a little secret chamber, which no one knew of but himself, and there he made a poisonous apple. Outwardly it looked beautiful, white with red cheeks, so that everyone who saw it longed to eat it, but anyone who might do so would certainly die on the spot. When the apple was quite finished he stained his face and dressed himself up as a peasant, and so he went over the seven hills to the seven Dwarfs. He knocked at the door, as usual, but Snowdrop put his head out of the window and called out:

"I may not let anyone in, the seven Dwarfs have forbidden me to do so."

"Are you afraid of being poisoned?" asked the old man. "See, I will cut this apple in half. I'll eat the white cheek and you can eat the red."

But the apple was so cunningly made that only the red cheek was poisonous. Snowdrop longed to eat the tempting fruit, and when he saw that the peasant man was eating it himself, he couldn't resist the temptation any longer, and stretching out his hand he took the poisonous half. But hardly had the first bite

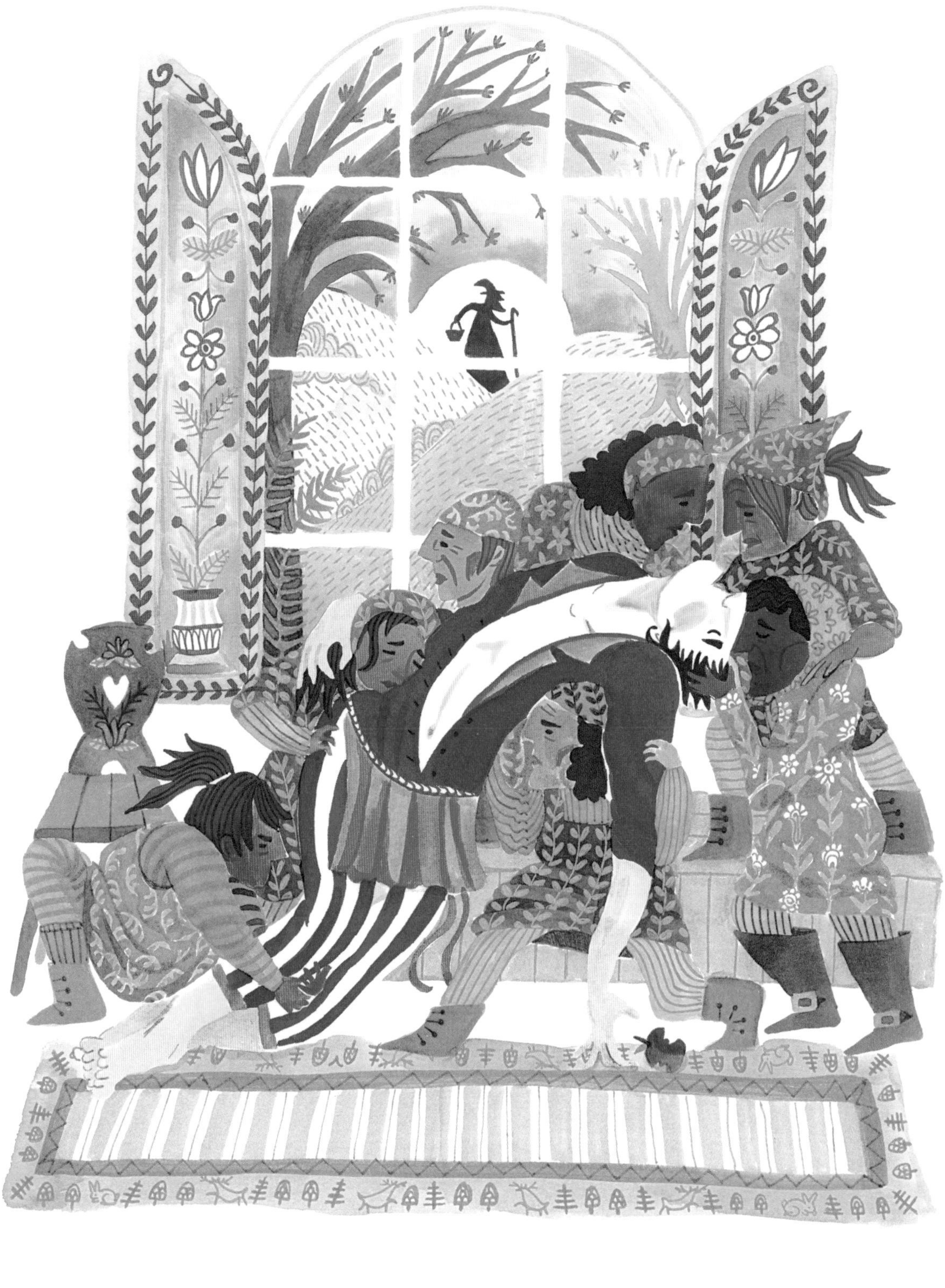

passed his lips than he fell down dead on the ground. Then the eyes of the cruel King sparkled with glee, and laughing aloud he cried:

"As white as snow, as red as blood, and as black as ebony, this time the Dwarfs won't be able to bring you back to life."

When he got home he asked the mirror:

"Mirror, mirror, hanging there, Who in all the land's most fair?" and this time it replied:

"You are most fair, my Gentleman King, None fairer in the land, I sing." Then his jealous heart was at rest – at least, as much at rest as a jealous heart can ever be.

When the little Dwarfs came home in the evening they found Snowdrop lying on the ground, and he neither breathed nor stirred. They lifted him up, and looked round everywhere to see if they could find anything poisonous about. They unlaced his shirt, combed his hair, washed him with water and wine, but all in vain; the child was dead and remained dead. Then they placed him on a bier, and all the seven Dwarfs sat round it, weeping and sobbing for three whole days. At last they made up their minds to bury him, but he looked as blooming as a living being, and his cheeks were still such a lovely colour, that they said:

"We can't hide him away in the black ground."

So they had a coffin made of transparent glass, and they laid him in it, and wrote on the lid in golden letters that he was a royal Prince. Then they put the coffin on the top of the mountain, and one of the Dwarfs always remained beside it and kept watch over it. And the very birds of the air came and bewailed Snowdrop's death, first an owl, and then a raven, and last of all a little dove.

Snowdrop lay a long time in the coffin, and he always looked the same, just as if he were fast asleep, and he remained as white as snow, as red as blood, and his hair as black as ebony.

Now it happened one day that a Princess came to the wood and passed by the Dwarfs' house. She saw the coffin on the hill, with the beautiful Snowdrop inside it, and when she had read what was written on it in golden letters, she said to the Dwarf:

"Give me the coffin. I'll give you whatever you like for it."

But the Dwarf said: "No; we wouldn't part with it for all the gold in the world."

"Well, then," she replied, "give it to me, because I can't live without Snowdrop. I will cherish and love it as my dearest possession."

She spoke so sadly that the good Dwarfs had pity on her, and gave her the coffin, and the Princess made her servants bear it away on their shoulders. Now it happened that as they were going down the hill they stumbled over a bush, and jolted the coffin so violently that the poisonous bit of apple Snowdrop had swallowed fell out of his throat. He gradually opened his eyes, lifted up the lid of the coffin, and sat up alive and well.

"Oh! dear me, where am I?" he cried.

The Princess answered joyfully, "You are with me," and she told him all that had happened, adding, "I love you better than anyone in the whole wide world. Will you come with me to my mother's palace and be my husband?"

Snowdrop consented, and went with her, and the marriage was celebrated with great pomp and splendour.

Now Snowdrop's wicked stepfather was one of the guests invited to the wedding feast. When he had dressed himself very gorgeously for the occasion, he went to the mirror, and said:

"Mirror, mirror, hanging there, Who in all the land's most fair?" and the mirror answered:

"My Gentleman King, you are fair, 'tis true, But Snowdrop is fairer far than you." When the wicked man heard these words he uttered a curse, and was beside himself with rage and mortification. At first he didn't want to go to the wedding at all, but at the same time he felt he would never be happy till he had seen the young King. As he entered Snowdrop recognised him, and nearly fainted with fear; but red-hot iron shoes had been prepared for the wicked old King, and he was made to get into them and dance till he fell down dead.

LITTLE RED RIDING HOOD

Once upon a time there lived in a certain village a little country boy, the prettiest creature was ever seen. His father was excessively fond of him; and his grandfather doted on him still more. This good man had made for him a little red riding-hood; which became the boy so extremely well that everybody called him Little Red Riding-Hood.

One day his father, having made some custards, said to him:

"Go, my dear, and see how thy grandpapa does, for I hear he has been very ill; carry him a custard, and this little pot of butter."

Little Red Riding-Hood set out immediately to go to his grandfather, who lived in another village.

As he was going through the wood, he met with Mistress Wolf, who had a very great mind to eat him up, but she durst not, because of some faggot-makers hard by in the forest. She asked him whither he was going. The poor child, who did not know that it was dangerous to stay and hear a wolf talk, said to her:

"I am going to see my grandpapa and carry him a custard and a little pot of butter from my papa."

"Does he live far off?" said the Wolf.

"Oh! ay," answered Little Red Riding-Hood; "it is beyond that mill you see there, at the first house in the village."

"Well," said the Wolf, "and I'll go and see him too. I'll go this way and you go that, and we shall see who will be there soonest."

The Wolf began to run as fast as she could, taking the nearest way, and the little boy went by that farthest about, diverting himself in gathering nuts, running after butterflies, and making nosegays of such little flowers as he met with. The Wolf was not long before she got to the old man's house. She knocked at the door – tap, tap.

"Who's there?"

"Your grandchild, Little Red Riding-Hood," replied the Wolf, counterfeiting his voice; "who has brought you a custard and a little pot of butter sent you by papa."

The good grandfather, who was in bed, because he was some-what ill, cried out:

"Pull the bobbin, and the latch will go up."

The Wolf pulled the bobbin, and the door opened, and then presently she fell upon the good man and ate him up in a moment, for it was above three days that she had not touched a bit. She then shut the door and went into the grandfather's bed, expecting Little Red Riding-Hood, who came some time afterwards and knocked at the door – tap, tap.

"Who's there?"

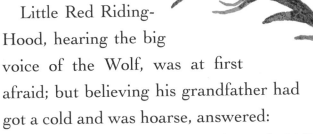

Little Red Riding-Hood, hearing the big voice of the Wolf, was at first afraid; but believing his grandfather had got a cold and was hoarse, answered:

"'Tis your grandchild, Little Red Riding-Hood, who has brought you a custard and a little pot of butter papa sends you."

The Wolf cried out to him, softening her voice as much as she could:

"Pull the bobbin, and the latch will go up."

Little Red Riding-Hood pulled the bobbin, and the door opened.

The Wolf, seeing him come in, said to him, hiding herself under the bedclothes:

"Put the custard and the little pot of butter upon the stool, and come and lie down with me."

Little Red Riding-Hood undressed himself and went into bed, where, being greatly amazed to see how his grandfather looked in his nightclothes, he said to him:

"Grandpapa, what great arms you have got!"

"That is the better to hug thee, my dear."

"Grandpapa, what great legs you have got!"

113

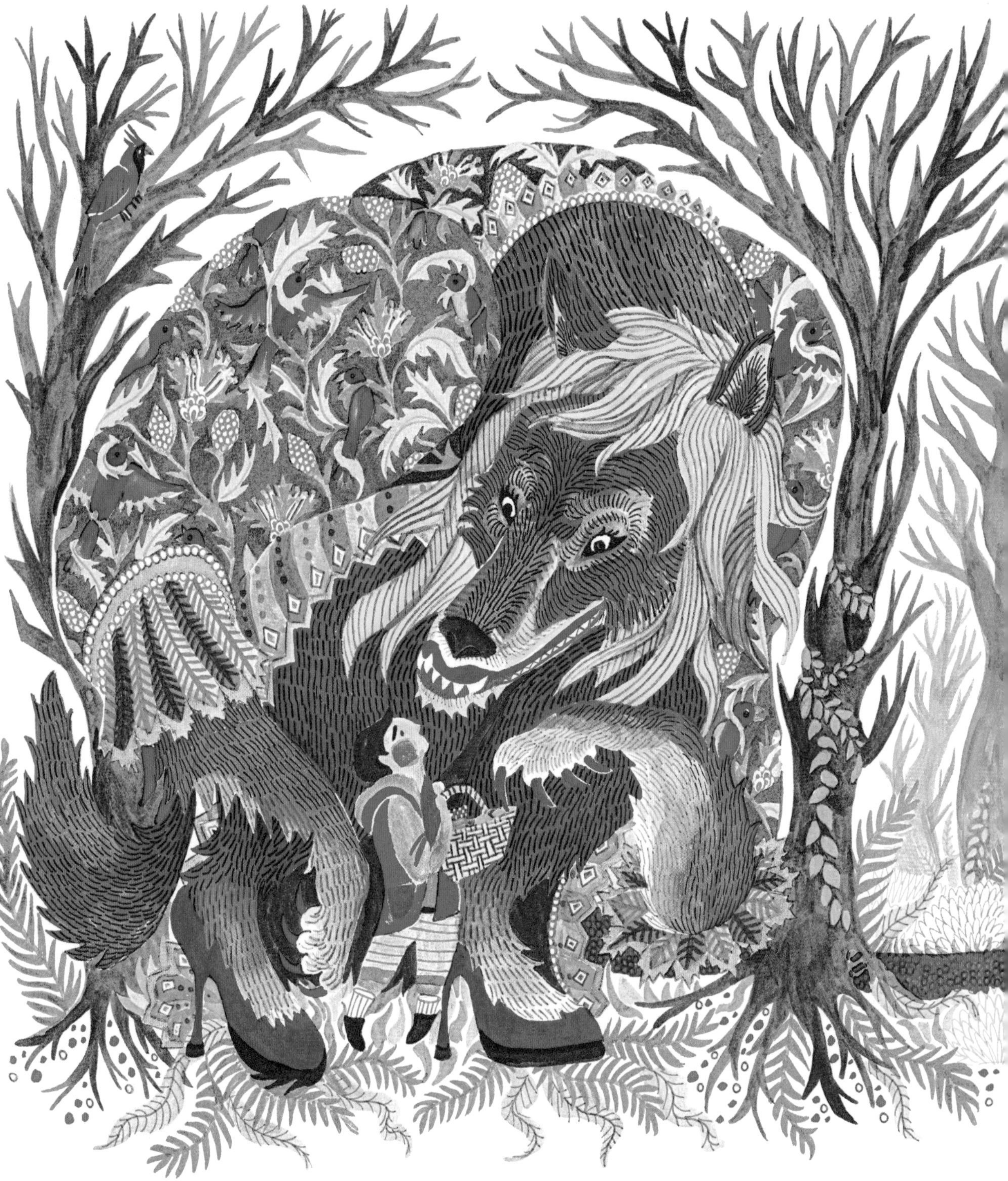

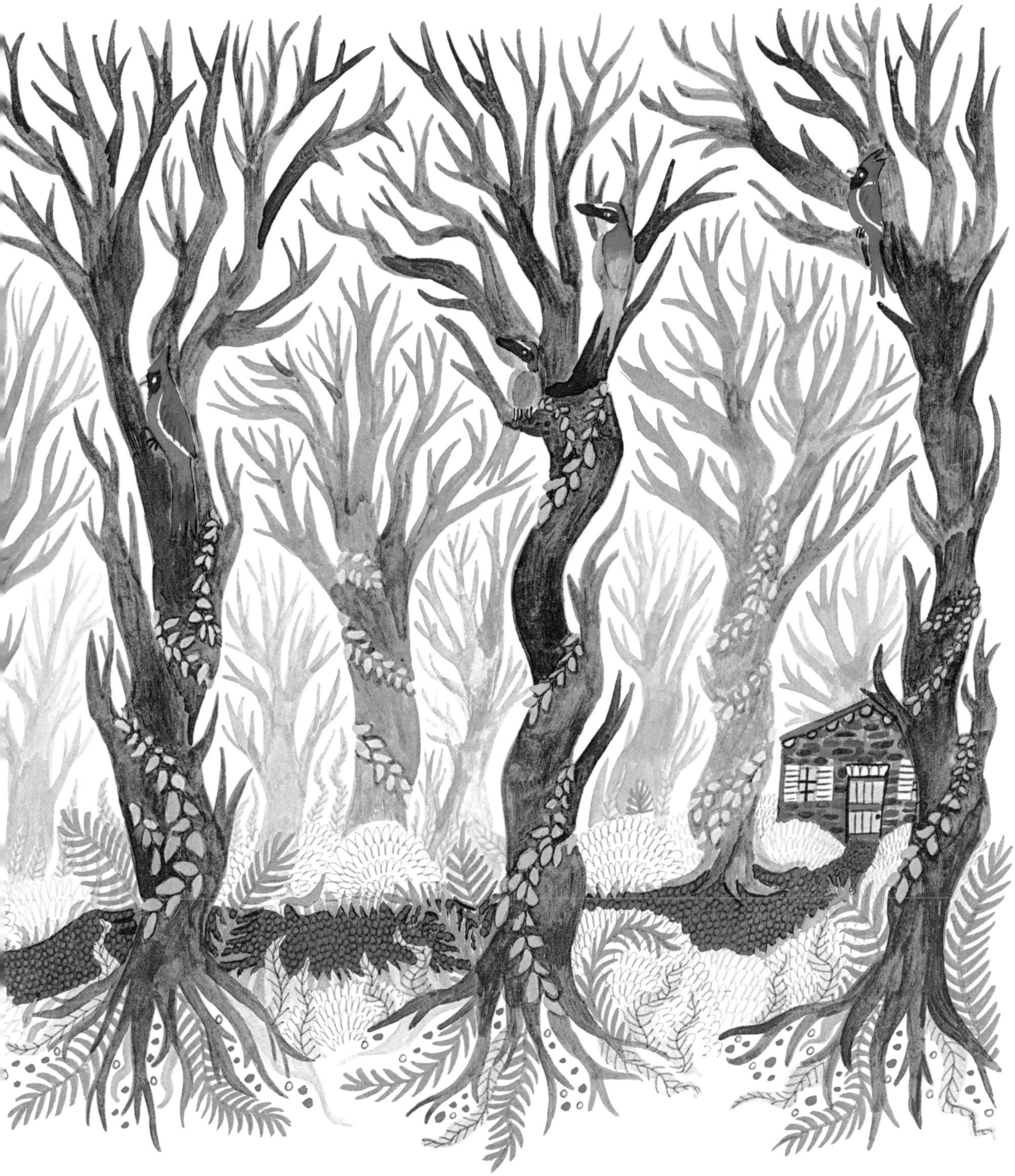

"That is to run the better, my child."

"Grandpapa, what great ears you have got!"

"That is to hear the better, my child."

"Grandpapa, what great eyes you have got!"

"It is to see the better, my child."

"Grandpapa, what great teeth you have got!"

"That is to eat thee up."

And, saying these words, this wicked wolf fell upon Little Red Riding-Hood, and ate him all up.

THE SLEEPING HANDSOME
IN THE WOOD

There were formerly a queen and a king, who were so sorry that they had no children; so sorry that it cannot be expressed. They went to all the waters in the world; vows, pilgrimages, all ways were tried, and all to no purpose.

At last, however, the King had a son. There was a very fine christening; and the Prince had for his godfathers all the fairies they could find in the whole queendom (they found seven), that every one of them might give him a gift, as was the custom of fairies in those days. By this means the Prince had all the perfections imaginable.

After the ceremonies of the christening were over, all the company returned to the Queen's palace, where was prepared a great feast for the fairies. There was placed before every one of them a magnificent cover with a case of massive gold, wherein were a spoon, knife, and fork, all of pure gold set with diamonds and rubies. But as they were all sitting down at table they saw come into the hall a very old fairy, whom they had not invited, because it was above fifty years since he had been out of a certain tower, and he was believed to be either dead or enchanted.

The Queen ordered him a cover, but could not furnish him with a case of gold as the others, because they had only seven made for the seven fairies. The old Fairy fancied he was slighted, and muttered some threats between his teeth. One of the young fairies who sat by him overheard how he grumbled; and, judging that he might give the little Prince some unlucky gift, went, as soon as they rose from table, and hid himself behind the hangings, that he might speak last, and repair, as much as he could, the evil which the old Fairy might intend.

In the meanwhile all the fairies began to give their gifts to the Prince. The youngest gave him the gift that he should be the most beautiful person in the world; the next, that he should have the wit of an angel; the third, that he should have a wonderful grace in everything he did; the fourth, that he should dance perfectly well; the fifth, that he should sing like a nightingale; and the sixth, that he should play all kinds of music to the utmost perfection.

The old Fairy's turn coming next, with a head shaking more with spite than age, he said that the Prince should have his hand pierced with a spindle and die of the wound. This terrible gift made the whole company tremble, and everybody fell a-crying.

At this very instant the young Fairy came out from behind the hangings, and spake these words aloud:

"Assure yourselves, O Queen and King, that your son shall not die of this disaster. It is true, I have no power to undo entirely what my elder has done. The Prince shall indeed pierce his hand with a spindle; but, instead of dying, he shall only fall into a profound sleep, which shall last a hundred years, at the expiration of which a queen's daughter shall come and awake him."

The Queen, to avoid the misfortune foretold by the old Fairy, caused immediately proclamation to be made, whereby everybody was forbidden, on pain of death, to spin with a distaff and spindle, or to have so much as any spindle in their houses. About fifteen or sixteen years after, the Queen and King being gone to one of their houses of pleasure, the young Prince happened one day to divert himself in running up and down the palace; when going up from one apartment to another, he came into a little room on the top of the tower, where a good old man, alone, was spinning with his spindle. This good man had never heard of the Queen's proclamation against spindles.

"What are you doing there, goody?" said the Prince.

"I am spinning, my pretty child," said the old man, who did not know who he was.

"Ha!" said the Prince, "this is very pretty; how do you do it? Give it to me, that I may see if I can do so."

He had no sooner taken it into his hand than, whether being very hasty at it, somewhat unhandy, or that the decree of the Fairy had so ordained it, it ran into his hand, and he fell down in a swoon.

The good old man, not knowing very well what to do in this affair, cried out for help. People came in from every quarter in great numbers; they threw water upon the Prince's face, unlaced him, struck him on the palms of his hands, and rubbed his temples with Hungary-water; but nothing would bring him to himself.

And now the Queen, who came up at the noise, bethought herself of the prediction of the fairies, and, judging very well that this must necessarily come to pass, since the fairies had said it, caused the Prince to be carried into the finest apartment in her palace, and to be laid upon a bed all embroidered with gold and silver.

One would have taken him for a little angel, he was so very beautiful; for his swooning away had not diminished one bit of his complexion; his cheeks were carnation, and his lips were coral; indeed, his eyes were shut, but he was heard to breathe softly, which satisfied those about him that he was not dead. The Queen commanded that they should not disturb him, but let him sleep quietly till his hour of awaking was come.

The good Fairy who had saved his life by condemning him to sleep a hundred years was in the queendom of Matakin, twelve thousand leagues off, when this accident befell the Prince; but he was instantly informed of it by a little dwarf, who had boots of seven leagues, that is, boots with which she could tread over seven leagues of ground in one stride. The Fairy came away immediately, and he arrived, about an hour after, in a fiery chariot drawn by dragons.

The Queen handed him out of the chariot, and he approved everything she had done; but as he had very great foresight, he thought when the Prince should awake he might not know what to do with himself, being all alone in this old palace; and this was what he did: he touched with his wand everything in the palace (except the Queen and King) – governors, men of honour, gentlemen of the bedchamber, ladies, officers, stewards, cooks, undercooks, scullions, guards, with their beefeaters, pages, footwomen; he likewise touched all the horses which were in the stables, as well pads as others, the great dogs in the outward court and pretty little Mopsey too, the Prince's little spaniel, which lay by him on the bed.

Immediately upon his touching them they all fell asleep, that they might not awake before their master and that they might be ready to wait upon him when he wanted them. The very spits at the fire, as full as they could hold of partridges and pheasants, did fall asleep also. All this was done in a moment. Fairies are not long in doing their business.

And now the Queen and the King, having kissed their dear child without waking him, went out of the palace and put forth a proclamation that nobody should dare to come near it.

This, however, was not necessary, for in a quarter of an hour's time there grew up all round about the park such a vast number of trees, great and small, bushes and brambles, twining one within another, that neither woman nor beast could pass through; so that nothing could be seen but the very top of the towers of the palace; and that, too, not unless it was a good way off. Nobody doubted but the Fairy gave herein a very extraordinary sample of his art, that the Prince, while he continued sleeping, might have nothing to fear from any curious people.

When a hundred years were gone and passed the daughter of the Queen then reigning, and who was of another family from that of the sleeping Prince, being gone a-hunting on that side of the country, asked:

What those towers were which she saw in the middle of a great thick wood?

Everyone answered according as they had heard. Some said:

That it was a ruinous old castle, haunted by spirits.

Others, that all the sorceresses and wizards of the country kept there their Sabbath or night's meeting.

The common opinion was: That an ogress lived there, and that she carried thither all the little children she could catch, that she might eat them up at her leisure, without anybody being able to follow her, as having herself only the power to pass through the wood.

The Princess was at a stand, not knowing what to believe, when a very good countrywoman spake to her thus:

"May it please your royal highness, it is now about fifty years since I heard from my mother, who heard my grandmother say, that there was then in this castle a prince, the most beautiful was ever seen; that he must sleep there a hundred years, and should be waked by a queen's daughter, for whom he was reserved."

The young Princess was all on fire at these words, believing, without weighing the matter, that she could put an end to this rare adventure; and, pushed on by love and honour, resolved that moment to look into it.

Scarce had she advanced towards the wood when all the great trees, the bushes, and brambles gave way of themselves to let her pass through; she walked up to the castle, which she saw at the end of a large avenue that she went into; and what a little surprised her was that she saw none of her people could follow her, because the trees closed again as soon as she had passed through them. However, she did not cease from continuing her way; a young and amorous princess is always valiant.

She came into a spacious outward court, where everything she saw might have frozen up the most fearless person with horror. There reigned over all a most frightful silence; the image of death everywhere showed itself, and there was nothing to be seen but stretched-out bodies of women and animals, all seeming to be dead. She, however, very well knew, by the ruby faces and pimpled noses of the beefeaters, that they were only asleep; and their goblets, wherein still remained some drops of wine, showed plainly that they fell asleep in their cups.

She then crossed a court paved with marble, went up the stairs, and came into the guard chamber, where guards were standing in their ranks, with their muskets upon their shoulders, and snoring as loud as they could. After that she went through several rooms full of ladies and gentlemen, all asleep, some standing, others sitting. At last she came into a chamber all gilded with gold, where she saw upon a bed, the curtains of which were all open, the finest sight was ever beheld – a prince, who appeared to be about fifteen or sixteen years of age, and whose bright and, in a manner, resplendent beauty, had somewhat in it divine. She approached with trembling and admiration, and fell down before him upon her knees.

And now, as the enchantment was at an end, the Prince

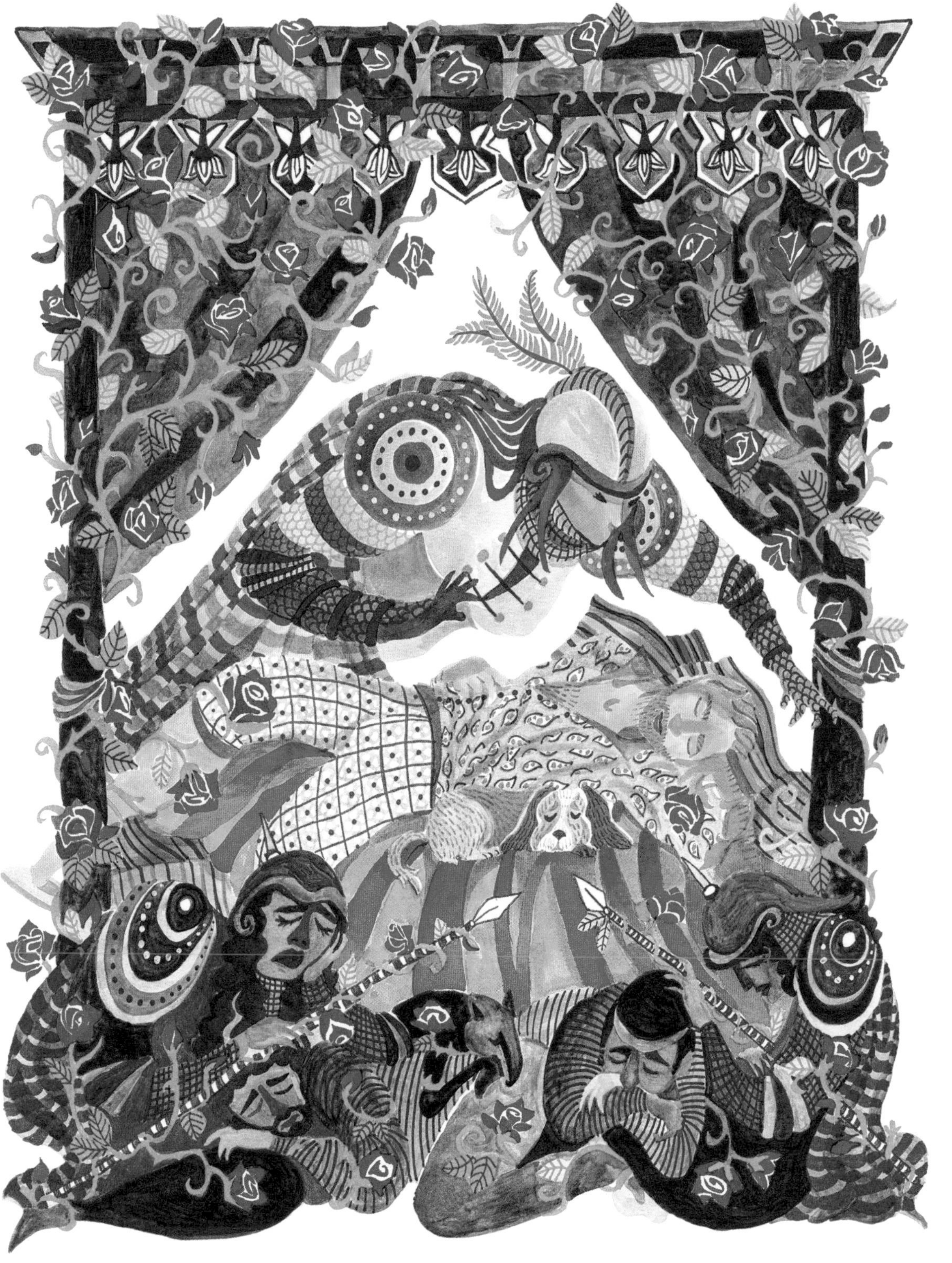

awaked, and looking on her with eyes more tender than the first view might seem to admit of:

"Is it you, my Princess?" said he to her. "You have waited a long while."

The Princess, charmed with these words, and much more with the manner in which they were spoken, knew not how to show her joy and gratitude; she assured him that she loved him better than she did herself; their discourse was not well connected, they did weep more than talk – little eloquence, a great deal of love. She was more at a loss than he, and we need not wonder at it; he had time to think on what to say to her; for it is very probable (though history mentions nothing of it) that the good Fairy, during so long a sleep, had given him very agreeable dreams. In short, they talked four hours together, and yet they said not half what they had to say.

In the meanwhile all the palace awaked; everyone thought upon their particular business, and as all of them were not in love they were ready to die for hunger. The chief gentleman of honour, being as sharp set as other folks, grew very impatient, and told the Prince aloud that supper was served up. The Princess helped the Prince to rise; he was entirely dressed, and very magnificently, but her royal highness took care not to tell him that he was dressed like her great-grandfather, and had a point band peeping over a high collar; he looked not a bit the less charming and beautiful for all that.

They went into the great hall of looking glasses, where they supped, and were served by the Prince's officers, the violins and hautgirls played old tunes, but very excellent, though it was now above a hundred years since they had played; and after supper, without losing any time, the lady almoner married them in the chapel of the castle, and the chief gentleman of honour drew the curtains. They had but very little sleep – the Prince had no occasion; and the Princess left him next morning to return into the city, where her mother must needs have been in pain for her. The Princess told her:

That she lost her way in the forest as she was hunting, and that she had lain in the cottage of a charcoal-burner, who gave her cheese and brown bread.

The Queen, her mother, who was a good woman, believed her; but her father could not be persuaded it was true; and seeing that she went almost every day a-hunting, and that she always had some excuse ready for so doing, though she had lain out three or four nights together, he began to suspect that she was married, for she lived with the Prince above two whole years, and had by him two children, the eldest of which, who was a son, was named Morning, and the youngest, who was a daughter, they called Day, because she was a great deal hand-somer and more beautiful than her brother.

The King spoke several times to his daughter, to inform him-self after what manner she did pass her time, and that in this she ought in duty to satisfy him. But she never dared to trust him with her secret; she feared him, though she loved him, for he was of the race of the Ogres, and the Queen would never have married him had it not been for his vast riches; it was even whispered about the Court that he had Ogreish inclinations, and that, whenever he saw little children passing by, he had all the difficulty in the world to avoid falling upon them. And so the Princess would never tell him one word.

But when the Queen was dead, which happened about two years afterwards, and she saw herself lady and mistress, she openly declared her marriage; and she went in great ceremony to conduct her King to the palace. They made a magnificent entry into the capital city, he riding between his two children.

Soon after the Queen went to make war with the Empress Contalabutte, her neighbour. She left the government of the queendom to the King her father, and earnestly recommended to his care her husband and children. She was obliged to continue her expedition all the summer, and as soon as she departed the King-father sent his son-in-law to a country house among the woods, that he might with the more ease gratify his horrible longing.

Some few days afterwards he went thither himself, and said to his clerk of the kitchen:

"I have a mind to eat little Morning for my dinner tomorrow."

"Ah! Sir," cried the clerk of the kitchen.

"I will have it so," replied the King (and this he spoke in the tone of an Ogre who had a strong desire to eat fresh meat), "and will eat him with a *sauce Roberta*."

The poor woman, knowing very well that she must not play tricks with Ogres, took her great knife and went up into little Morning's chamber. He was then four years old, and came up to her jumping and laughing, to take her about the neck, and ask her for some sugar-candy. Upon which she began to weep, the great knife fell out of her hand, and she went into the back yard, and killed a little lamb, and dressed it with such good sauce that her master assured her that he had never eaten anything so good in his life. She had at the same time taken up little Morning, and carried him to her husband, to conceal him in the lodging she had at the bottom of the courtyard.

About eight days afterwards the wicked King said to the clerk of the kitchen, "I will sup on little Day."

She answered not a word, being resolved to cheat him as she had done before. She went to find out little Day, and saw her with a little foil in her hand, with which she was fencing with a great monkey, the child being then only three years of age. She took her up in her arms and carried her to her husband, that he might conceal her in his chamber along with her brother, and

131

in the room of little Day cooked up a young kid, very tender, which the Ogre found to be wonderfully good.

This was hitherto all mighty well; but one evening this wicked Ogre King said to his clerk of the kitchen:

"I will eat the King with the same sauce I had with his children."

It was now that the poor clerk of the kitchen despaired of being able to deceive him. The young King was turned of twenty, not reckoning the hundred years he had been asleep; and how to find in the yard a beast so firm was what puzzled her. She took then a resolution, that she might save her own life, to cut the King's throat; and going up into his chamber, with intent to do it at once, she put herself into as great a fury as she could possibly, and came into the young King's room with her dagger in her hand. She would not, however, surprise him, but told him, with a great deal of respect, the orders she had received from the King-father.

"Do it; do it" (said he, stretching out his neck). "Execute your orders, and then I shall go and see my children, my poor children, whom I so much and so tenderly loved."

For he thought them dead ever since they had been taken away without his knowledge.

"No, no, sir," (cried the poor clerk of the kitchen, all in tears); "you shall not die, and yet you shall see your children again; but then you must go home with me to my lodgings, where I have concealed them, and I shall deceive the King once more, by giving him in your stead a young hind."

Upon this she forthwith conducted him to her chamber, where, leaving him to embrace his children, and cry along with them, she went and dressed a young hind, which the King had for his supper, and devoured it with the same appetite as if it had been the young King. Exceedingly was he delighted with his cruelty, and he had invented a story to tell the Queen, at her return, how the mad wolves had eaten up the King her husband and his two children.

One evening, as he was, according to his custom, rambling round about the courts and yards of the palace to see if he could smell any fresh meat, he heard, in a ground room, little Day crying, for her papa was going to whip her, because she had been naughty; and he heard, at the same time, little Morning begging pardon for his sister.

The Ogre presently knew the voice of the King and his children, and being quite mad that he had been thus deceived, he commanded next morning, by break of day (with a most horrible voice, which made everybody tremble), that they should bring into the middle of the great court a large tub, which he caused to be filled with toads, vipers, snakes, and all sorts of serpents, in order to have thrown into it the King and his children, the clerk of the kitchen, her husband and servant; all whom he had given orders should be brought thither with their hands tied behind them.

They were brought out accordingly, and the executioners were just going to throw them into the tub, when the Queen (who was not so soon expected) entered the court on horseback (for she came post) and asked, with the utmost astonishment, what was the meaning of that horrible spectacle.

No one dared to tell her, when the Ogre, all enraged to see what had happened, threw himself head foremost into the tub, and was instantly devoured by the ugly creatures he had ordered to be thrown into it for others. The Queen could not but be very sorry, for he was her father; but she soon comforted herself with her beautiful husband and her pretty children.

FRAU RUMPELSTILTZKIN

There was once upon a time a poor miller who had a very beautiful son. Now it happened one day that she had an audience with the Queen, and in order to appear a person of some importance she told her that she had a son who could spin straw into gold. "Now that's a talent worth having," said the Queen to the miller; "if your son is as clever as you say, bring him to my palace tomorrow, and I'll put him to the test." When the boy was brought to her she led him into a room full of straw, gave him a spinning wheel and spindle, and said: "Now set to work and spin all night till early dawn, and if by that time you haven't spun the straw into gold you shall die." Then she closed the door behind her and left him alone inside.

So the poor miller's son sat down, and didn't know what in the world he was to do. He hadn't the least idea of how to spin straw into gold, and became at last so miserable that he began to cry. Suddenly the door opened, and in stepped a tiny little woman and said: "Good evening, Mr Miller-lad; why are you crying so bitterly?" "Oh!" answered the boy, "I have to spin straw into gold, and haven't a notion how it's done." "What will you give me if I spin it for you?" asked the tiny woman. "My necklace," replied the boy. The little woman took the necklace, sat herself down at the wheel, and whir, whir, whir, the wheel went round three times, and the bobbin was full. Then she put on another, and whir, whir, whir, the wheel went round three times, and the second too was full; and so it went on till the morning, when all the straw was spun away, and all the bobbins were full of gold. As soon as the sun rose the Queen came, and when she perceived the gold she was astonished and delighted, but her heart only lusted more than ever after the precious metal. She had the miller's son put into another room full of straw, much bigger than the first, and bade him, if he valued his life, spin it all into gold before the following morning. The boy didn't know what to do, and began to cry; then the door opened as before, and the tiny little woman appeared and said: "What'll you give me if I spin the straw into gold for you?" "The ring from my finger," answered the boy. The tiny woman took the ring, and whir! round went the spinning wheel again, and when morning broke she had spun all the straw into glittering gold. The Queen was pleased beyond measure at the sight but her greed for gold was still not satisfied, and she had the miller's son brought into a yet bigger room full of straw, and said: "You must spin all this away in the night; but if you succeed this time you shall become my husband." "He's only a miller's son, it's true," she thought; "but I couldn't find a richer husband if I were to search the whole world over." When the boy was alone the little woman appeared for the third time, and said: "What'll you give me if I spin the straw for you once again?" "I've nothing more to give," answered the boy. "Then promise me when you are King to give me your first child." "Who knows what mayn't happen before that?" thought the miller's son; and besides, he saw no other way out of it, so he promised the little woman what she demanded, and she set to work once more and spun the straw into gold. When the Queen came in the morning, and found everything as she had desired, she straightway made him her husband, and the miller's son became a king.

When a year had passed a beautiful daughter was born to him, and the King thought no more of the little woman, till all of a sudden one day she stepped into his room and said: "Now give me what you promised." The King was in a great state, and offered the little woman all the riches in his queendom if she would only leave him the child. But the tiny woman said: "No, a living creature is dearer to me than all the treasures in the world." Then the King began to cry and sob so bitterly that the little woman was sorry for him, and said: "I'll give you three days to guess my name, and if you find it out in that time you may keep your child."

Then the King pondered the whole night over all the names he had ever heard, and sent a messenger to scour the land, and to pick up far and near any names she should come across. When the little woman arrived on the following day he began with Kasandra, Melkiorine, Bellarosa and all the other names he knew, in a string, but at each one the tiny woman called out: "That's not my name." The next day he sent to inquire the names of all the people in the neighbourhood, and had a long list of the most uncommon and extraordinary for the little woman when she made her appearance. "Is your name, perhaps, Sheepshanks, Cruickshanks, Spindleshanks?" but she always replied: "That's not my name." On the third day the messenger returned and announced: "I have not been able to find any new names, but as I came upon a high hill round the corner of the wood, where the foxes and hares bid each other good night, I saw a little house, and in front of the house burned a fire, and round the fire sprang the most grotesque little woman, hopping on one leg and crying:

"Tomorrow I brew, today I bake, and then the child away I'll take; For the King will not proclaim, that Rumpelstiltzkin is my name!"

You can imagine the King's delight at hearing the name, and when the little woman stepped in shortly afterwards and asked:

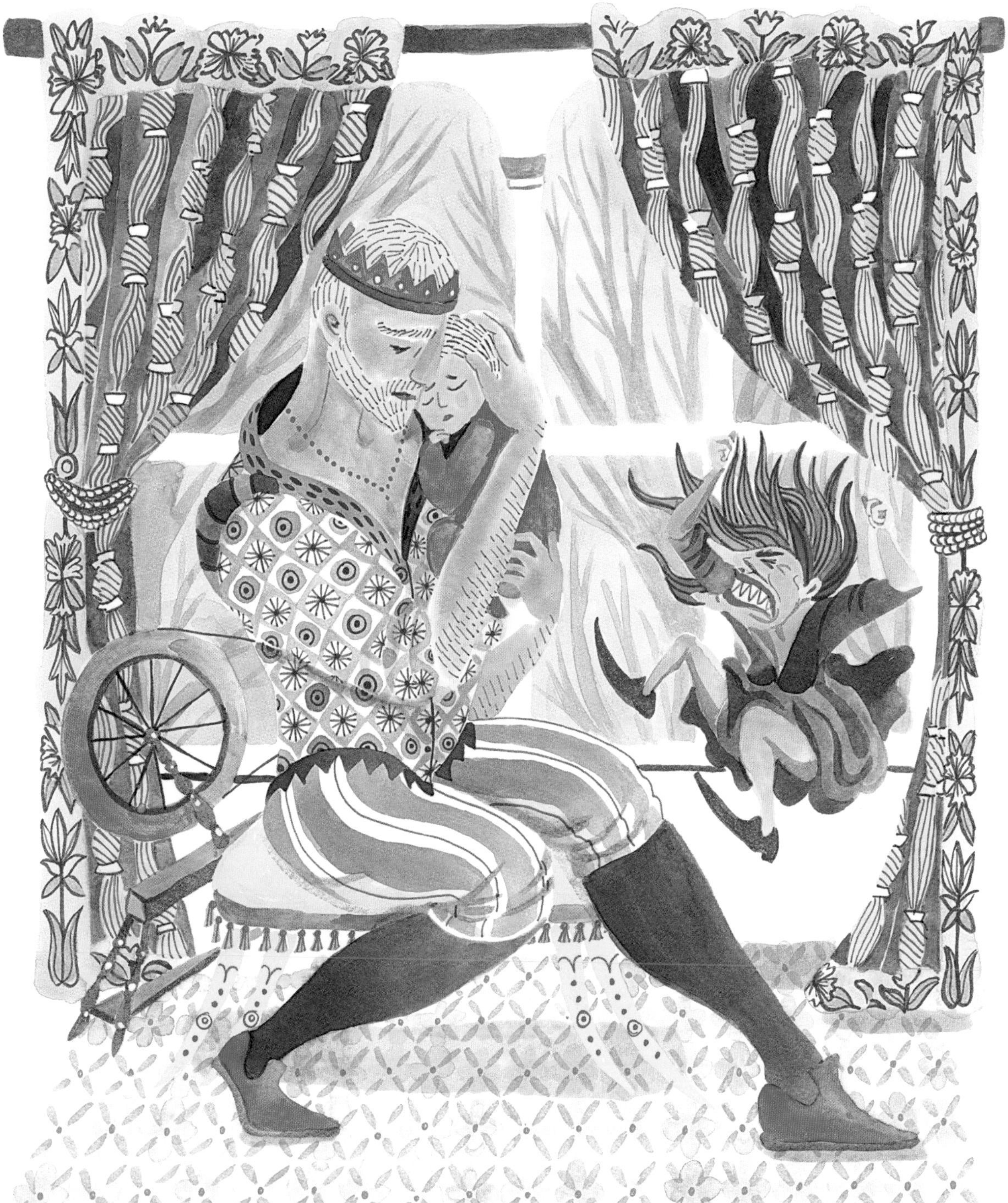

"Now, my gentleman King, what's my name?" he asked first: "Is your name Concetta?" "No." "Is your name Harriet?" "No." "Is your name, perhaps, Rumpelstiltzkin?" "Some demon has told you that, some demon has told you that," screamed the little woman, and in her rage drove her right foot so far into the ground that it sank in up to her waist; then in a passion she seized the left foot with both hands and tore herself in two.

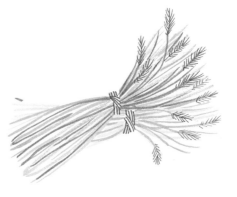

MISTRESS PUSS IN BOOTS

There was a miller who left no more estate to the three daughters she had than her mill, her ass, and her cat. The partition was soon made. Neither the scrivener nor attorney was sent for. They would soon have eaten up all the poor inheritance. The eldest had the mill, the second the ass, and the youngest nothing but the cat. The poor young lass was quite comfortless at having so poor a lot.

"My sisters", said she, "may get their living handsomely enough by joining their stocks together; but for my part, when I have eaten up my cat, and made me a muff of her skin, I must die of hunger."

The Cat, who heard all this, but made as if she did not, said to her with a grave and serious air:

"Do not thus afflict yourself, my good mistress. You have nothing else to do but to give me a bag and get a pair of boots made for me that I may scamper through the dirt and the brambles, and you shall see that you have not so bad a portion in me as you imagine."

The Cat's mistress did not build very much upon what she said. She had, however, often seen her play a great many cunning tricks to catch rats and mice, as when she used to hang by the heels, or hide herself in the meal, and make as if she were dead; so that she did not altogether despair of her affording her some help in her miserable condition. When the Cat had what she asked for, she booted herself very gallantly, and putting her bag about her neck, she held the strings of it in her two forepaws and went into a warren where was great abundance of rabbits. She put bran and sow-thistle into her bag, and stretching out at length, as if she had been dead, she waited for some young rabbits, not yet acquainted with the deceits of the world, to come and rummage her bag for what she had put into it.

Scarce was she lain down but she had what she wanted: a rash and foolish young rabbit jumped into her bag, and Madam Puss, immediately drawing close the strings, took and killed her without pity. Proud of her prey, she went with it to the palace and asked to speak with Her Majesty. She was shown upstairs into the Queen's apartment, and, making a low reverence, said to her:

"I have brought you, ma'am, a rabbit of the warren, which my noble lady the Marchioness of Carabas" (for that was the title which puss was pleased to give her mistress) "has commanded me to present to Your Majesty from her."

"Tell thy mistress", said the Queen, "that I thank her and that she does me a great deal of pleasure."

Another time she went and hid herself among some standing corn, holding still her bag open; and when a brace of partridges ran into it she drew the strings and so caught them both. She went and made a present of these to the Queen, as she had done before of the rabbit which she took in the warren. The Queen, in like manner, received the partridges with great pleasure, and ordered her some money, to drink.

The Cat continued for two or three months thus to carry her Majesty, from time to time, game of her mistress's taking. One day in particular, when she knew for certain that she was to take the air along the riverside, with her son, the most beautiful prince in the world, she said to her mistress:

"If you will follow my advice your fortune is made. You have nothing else to do but go and wash yourself in the river, in that part I shall show you, and leave the rest to me."

The Marchioness of Carabas did what the Cat advised her to, without knowing why or wherefore. While she was washing the Queen passed by, and the Cat began to cry out:

"Help! help! My Lady Marchioness of Carabas is going to be drowned."

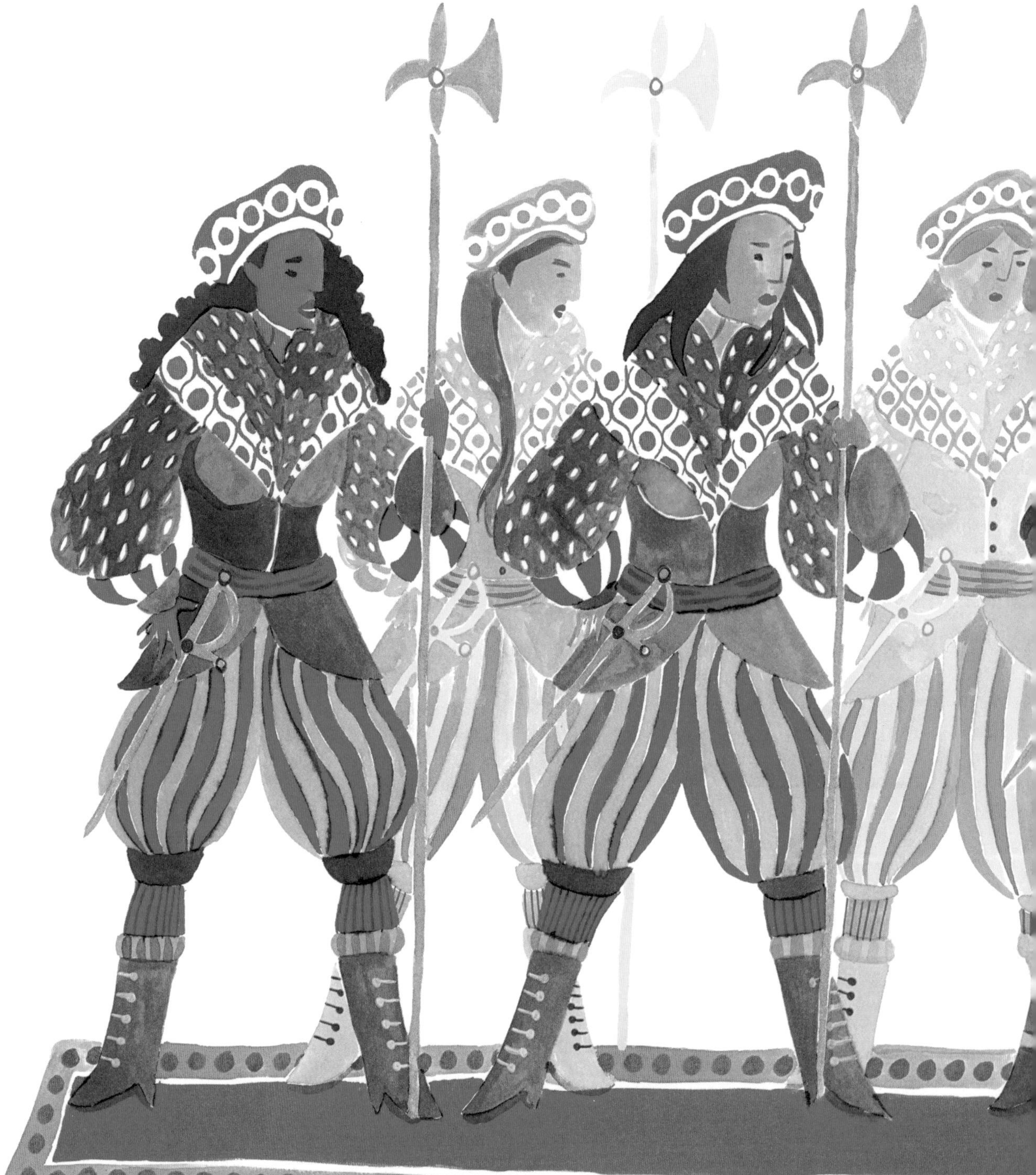

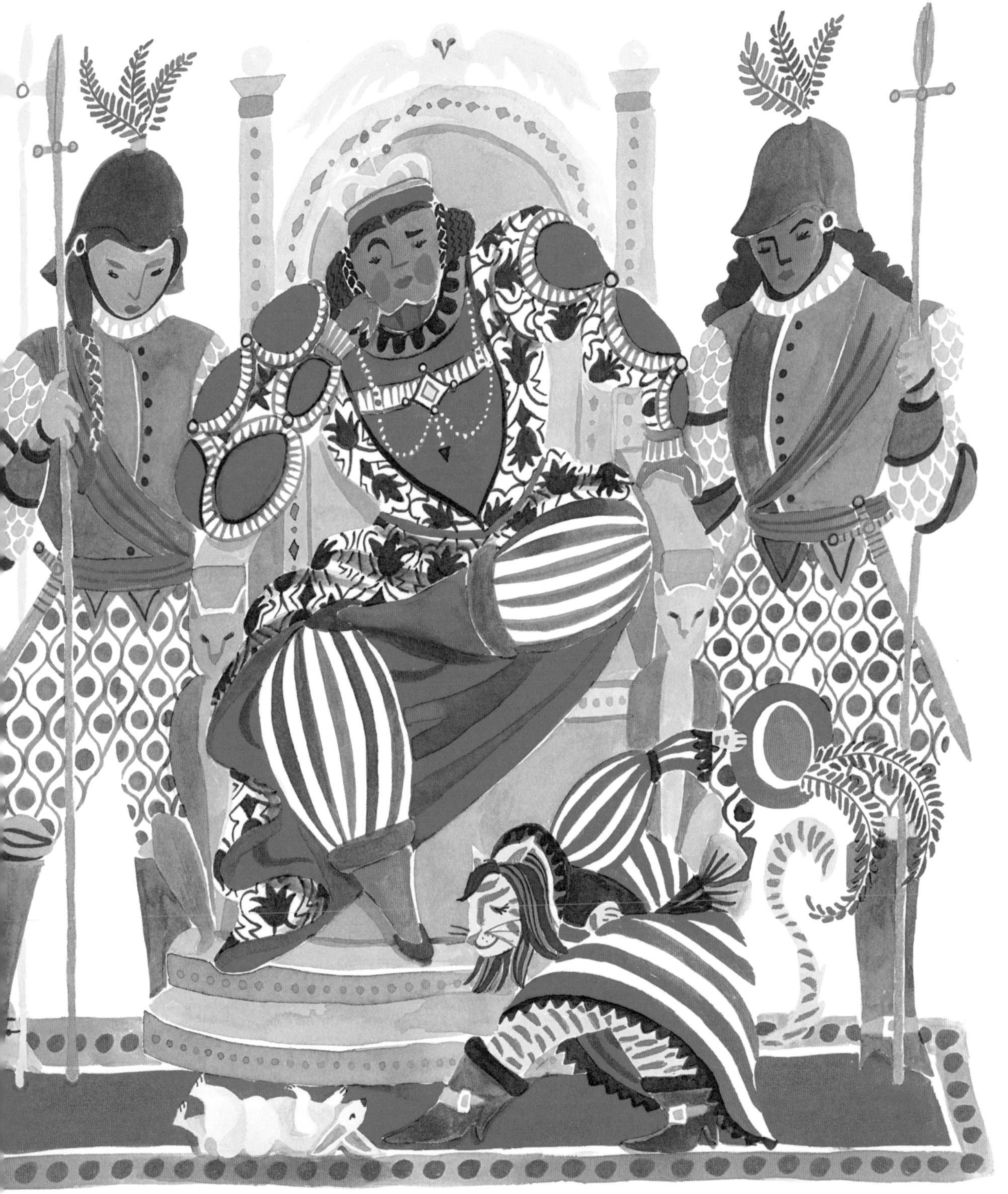

At this noise the Queen put her head out of the coach window, and, finding it was the Cat who had so often brought her such good game, she commanded her guards to run immediately to the assistance of her Ladyship the Marchioness of Carabas. While they were drawing the poor Marchioness out of the river, the Cat came up to the coach and told the Queen that, while her mistress was washing, there came by some rogues, who went off with her clothes, though she had cried out: "Thieves! thieves!" several times, as loud as she could.

This cunning Cat had hidden them under a great stone. The Queen immediately commanded the officers of her wardrobe to run and fetch one of her best dresses for the Lady Marchioness of Carabas.

The Queen caressed her after a very extraordinary manner, and as the fine clothes she had given her extremely set off her good mien (for she was well made and very handsome in her person), the Queen's son took a secret inclination to her, and the Marchioness of Carabas had no sooner cast two or three respectful and somewhat tender glances but he fell in love with her to distraction. The Queen would needs have her come into the coach and take part of the airing. The Cat, quite overjoyed to see her project begin to succeed, marched on before, and, meeting with some countrywomen, who were mowing a meadow, she said to them:

"Good people, you who are mowing, if you do not tell the Queen that the meadow you mow belongs to my Lady Marchioness of

Carabas, you shall be chopped as small as herbs for the pot."

The Queen did not fail asking of the mowers to whom the meadow they were mowing belonged.

"To my Lady Marchioness of Carabas," answered they altogether, for the Cat's threats had made them terribly afraid.

"You see, ma'am," said the Marchioness, "this is a meadow which never fails to yield a plentiful harvest every year."

The Mistress Cat, who went still on before, met with some reapers, and said to them:

"Good people, you who are reaping, if you do not tell the Queen that all this corn belongs to the Marchioness of Carabas, you shall be chopped as small as herbs for the pot."

The Queen, who passed by a moment after, would needs know to whom all that corn, which she then saw, did belong.

"To my Lady Marchioness of Carabas," replied the reapers, and the Queen was very well pleased with it, as well as the Marchioness, whom she congratulated thereupon. The Mistress Cat, who went always before, said the same words to all she met, and the Queen was astonished at the vast estates of my Lady Marchioness of Carabas.

Madam Puss came at last to a stately castle, the mistress of which was an ogress, the richest had ever been known; for all the lands which the Queen had then gone over belonged to this castle. The Cat, who had taken care to inform herself who this ogress was and what she could do, asked to speak with her, saying she could not pass so near her castle without having the honour of paying her respects to her.

The ogress received her as civilly as an ogress could do, and made her sit down.

"I have been assured", said the Cat, "that you have the gift of being able to change yourself into all sorts of creatures you have a mind to; you can, for example, transform yourself into a lion, or elephant, and the like."

"That is true," answered the ogress very briskly; "and to convince you, you shall see me now become a lion."

Puss was so sadly terrified at the sight of a lion so near her that she immediately got into the gutter, not without abundance of trouble and danger, because of her boots, which were of no use at all to her in walking upon the tiles. A little while after, when Puss saw that the ogress had resumed her natural form, she came down, and owned she had been very much frightened.

"I have been, moreover, informed," said the Cat, "but I know not how to believe it, that you have also the power to take on the shape of the smallest animals; for example, to change yourself into a rat or a mouse; but I must own to you I take this to be impossible."

"Impossible!" cried the ogress; "you shall see that presently."

And at the same time she changed herself into a mouse, and began to run about the floor. Puss no sooner perceived this but she fell upon her and ate her up.

Meanwhile the Queen, who saw, as she passed, this fine castle of the ogress's, had a mind to go into it. Puss, who heard the noise of her Majesty's coach running over the drawbridge, ran out, and said to the Queen:

"Your Majesty is welcome to this castle of my Lady Marchioness of Carabas."

"What! my Lady Marchioness," cried the Queen, "and does this castle also belong to you? There can be nothing finer than this court and all the stately buildings which surround it; let us go into it, if you please."

The Marchioness gave her hand to the Prince, and followed the Queen, who went first. They passed into a spacious hall, where they found a magnificent collation, which the ogress had prepared for her friends, who were that very day to visit her, but dared not to enter, knowing the Queen was there. Her Majesty was perfectly charmed with the good qualities of my Lady Marchioness of Carabas, as was her son, who had fallen violently in love with her, and, seeing the vast estate she possessed, said to her, after having drunk five or six glasses:

"It will be owing to yourself only, my Lady Marchioness, if you are not my daughter-in-law."

The Marchioness, making several low bows, accepted the honour which Her Majesty conferred upon her, and forthwith, that very same day, married the Prince.

Puss became a great Lady, and never ran after mice any more but only for her diversion.

THUMBELIN

There was once a man who wanted to have quite a tiny, little child, but he did not know where to get one from. So one day he went to an old Wizard and said to him: "I should so much like to have a tiny, little child; can you tell me where I can get one?"

"Oh, we have just got one ready!" said the Wizard. "Here is a barley-corn for you, but it's not the kind the farmer sows in her field, or feeds the hens and cocks with, I can tell you. Put it in a flowerpot, and then you will see something happen."

"Oh, thank you!" said the man, and gave the Wizard a shilling, for that was what it cost. Then he went home and planted the barley-corn; immediately there grew out of it a large and beautiful flower, which looked like a tulip, but the petals were tightly closed as if it were still only a bud.

"What a beautiful flower!" exclaimed the man, and he kissed the red and yellow petals; but as he kissed them the flower burst open. It was a real tulip, such as one can see any day; but in the middle of the blossom, on the green velvety petals, sat a little boy, quite tiny, trim, and pretty. He was scarcely half a thumb in height; so they called him Thumbelin. An elegant polished walnut shell served Thumbelin as a cradle, the blue petals of a violet were his mattress, and a rose leaf his coverlid. There he lay at night, but in the daytime he used to play about on the table; here the man had put a bowl, surrounded by a ring of flowers, with their stalks in water, in the middle of which floated a great tulip petal, and on this Thumbelin sat, and sailed from one side of the bowl to the other, rowing himself with two white horse hairs for oars. It was such a pretty sight! He could sing, too, with a voice more soft and sweet than had ever been heard before.

One night, when he was lying in his pretty little bed, an old toad crept in through a broken pane in the window. He was very ugly, clumsy, and clammy; he hopped on to the table where Thumbelin lay asleep under the red rose leaf.

'This would make a beautiful husband for my daughter,' said the toad, taking up the walnut shell, with Thumbelin inside, and hopping with it through the window into the garden.

There flowed a great wide stream, with slippery and marshy banks; here the toad lived with his daughter. Ugh! how ugly and clammy she was, just like her father! 'Croak, croak, croak!' was all she could say when she saw the pretty little boy in the walnut shell.

'Don't talk so loud, or you'll wake him,' said the old toad. 'He might escape us even now; he is as light as a feather. We will put him at once on a broad water lily leaf in the stream. That will be quite an island for him; he is so small and light. He can't run away from us there, whilst we are preparing the guest-chamber under the marsh where he shall live."

Outside in the brook grew many water lilies, with broad green leaves, which looked as if they were swimming about on the water.

The leaf farthest away was the largest, and to this the old toad swam with Thumbelin in his walnut shell.

The tiny Thumbelin woke up very early in the morning, and when he saw where he was he began to cry bitterly; for on every side of the great green leaf was water, and he could not get to the land.

The old toad was down under the marsh, decorating his room with rushes and yellow marigold leaves, to make it very grand for his new son-in-law; then he swam out with his ugly daughter to the leaf where Thumbelin lay. He wanted to fetch the pretty cradle to put it into his room before Thumbelin himself came there. The old toad bowed low in the water before him, and said: 'Here is my daughter; you shall marry her, and live in great magnificence down under the marsh.'

'Croak, croak, croak!' was all that the daughter could say. Then they took the neat little cradle and swam away with it; but Thumbelin sat alone on the great green leaf and wept, for he did not want to live with the clammy toad, or marry his ugly daughter. The little fishes swimming about under the water had seen the toad quite plainly, and heard what he had said; so they put up their heads to see the little boy. When they saw him, they thought him so pretty that they were very sorry he should go down with the ugly toad to live. No; that must not happen. They assembled in the water round the green stalk which supported the leaf on which he was sitting, and nibbled the stem in two. Away floated the leaf down the stream, bearing Thumbelin far beyond the reach of the toad.

On he sailed past several towns, and the little birds sitting in the bushes saw him, and sang, 'What a pretty little boy!' The leaf floated farther and farther away; thus Thumbelin left his native land.

A beautiful little white butterfly fluttered above him, and at last settled on the leaf. Thumbelin pleased her, and he, too, was delighted, for now the toads could not reach him, and it was so beautiful where he was travelling; the sun shone on the water and made it sparkle like the brightest silver. He took off his sash, and tied one end round the butterfly; the other end he fastened to the leaf, so that now it glided along with him faster than ever.

A great cockchafer came flying past; she caught sight of Thumbelin, and in a moment had put her arms round his slender waist, and had flown off with him to a tree. The green leaf floated away down the stream, and the butterfly with it, for she was fastened to the leaf and could not get loose from it. Oh, dear! How terrified poor little Thumbelin was when the cockchafer flew off with him to the tree! But he was especially distressed on the beautiful white butterfly's account, as he had tied her fast, so that if she could not get away she must starve to death. But the cockchafer did not trouble herself about that; she sat down with him on a large green leaf, gave him the honey out of the flowers to eat, and told him that he was very pretty, although he wasn't in the least like a cockchafer. Later on, all the other cockchafers who lived in the same tree came to pay calls; they examined Thumbelin closely, and remarked, "Why, he has only two legs! How very miserable!"

"He has no feelers!" cried another.

"How ugly he is!" said all the gentleman chafers – and yet Thumbelin was really very pretty.

The cockchafer who had stolen him knew this very well; but when she heard all the gentlemen saying he was ugly, she began to think so too, and would not keep him; he might go wherever he liked. So she flew down from the tree with him and put him on a daisy. There he sat and wept, because he was so ugly that the cockchafer would have nothing to do with him; and yet he was the most beautiful creature imaginable, so soft and delicate, like the loveliest rose leaf.

The whole summer poor little Thumbelin lived alone in the great wood. He plaited a bed for himself of blades of grass, and hung it up under a clover-leaf, so that he was protected from the rain; he gathered honey from the flowers for food, and drank the dew on the leaves every morning. Thus the summer and autumn passed, but then came winter – the long, cold winter. All the birds who had sung so sweetly about him had flown away; the trees shed their leaves, the flowers died; the great clover-leaf under which he had lived curled up, and nothing remained of it but the withered stalk. He was terribly cold, for his clothes were ragged, and he himself was so small and thin.

Poor little Thumbelin! He would surely be frozen to death. It began to snow, and every snowflake that fell on him was to him as a whole shovelful thrown on one of us, for we are so big, and he was only an inch high. He wrapt himself round in a dead leaf, but it was torn in the middle and gave him no warmth; he was trembling with cold.

Just outside the wood where he was now living lay a great cornfield. But the corn had been gone a long time; only the dry, bare stubble was left standing in the frozen ground. This made a forest for him to wander about in. All at once he came across the door of a field mouse, who had a little hole under a corn-stalk. There the mouse lived warm and snug, with a storeroom full of corn, a splendid kitchen and dining room. Poor little Thumbelin went up to the door and begged for a little piece of barley, for he had not had anything to eat for the last two days.

"Poor little creature!" said the field mouse, for he was a kind-hearted old thing at the bottom. "Come into my warm room and have some dinner with me."

As Thumbelin pleased him, he said: "As far as I am concerned you may spend the winter with me; but you must keep my room clean and tidy, and tell me stories, for I like that very much."

And Thumbelin did all that the kind old field mouse asked, and did it remarkably well too.

"Now I am expecting a visitor," said the field mouse; "my neighbour comes to call on me once a week. She is in better circumstances than I am, has great, big rooms, and wears a fine black-velvet coat. If you could only marry her, you would be well provided for. But she is blind. You must tell her all the prettiest stories you know."

But Thumbelin did not trouble his head about her, for she was only a mole. She came and paid them a visit in her black-velvet coat.

"She is so rich and so accomplished," the field mouse told him.

"Her house is twenty times larger than mine; she possesses great knowledge, but she cannot bear the sun and the beautiful flowers, and speaks slightingly of them, for she has never seen them."

Thumbelin had to sing to her, so he sang "Gentleman-bird, gentleman-bird, fly away home!" and other songs so prettily that the mole fell in love with him; but she did not say anything, she was a very cautious woman. A short time before she had dug a long passage through the ground from her own house to that of her neighbour; in this she gave the field mouse and Thumbelin permission to walk as often as they liked. But she begged them not to be afraid of the dead bird that lay in the passage: it was a real bird with beak and feathers, and must have died a little time ago, and now laid buried just where she had made her tunnel. The mole took a piece of rotten wood in her mouth, for that glows like fire in the dark, and went in front, lighting them through the long dark passage. When they came to the place where the dead bird lay, the mole put her broad nose against the ceiling and pushed a hole through, so that the daylight could shine down. In the middle of the path lay a dead swallow, her pretty wings pressed close to her sides, her claws and head drawn under her feathers; the poor bird had evidently died of cold. Thumbelin was very sorry, for he was very fond of all little birds; they had sung and twittered so beautifully to him all through the summer. But the mole kicked her with her bandy legs and said:

"Now she can't sing any more! It must be very miserable to be a little bird! I'm thankful that none of my little children are; birds always starve in winter."

"Yes, you speak like a sensible woman," said the field mouse. "What has a bird, in spite of all her singing, in the wintertime? She must starve and freeze, and that must be very pleasant for her, I must say!"

Thumbelin did not say anything; but when the other two had passed on he bent down to the bird, brushed aside the feathers from her head, and kissed her closed eyes gently. 'Perhaps it was she that sang to me so prettily in the summer,' he thought. "How much pleasure she did give me, dear little bird!"

The mole closed up the hole again which let in the light, and then escorted the gentlemen home. But Thumbelin could not sleep that night; so he got out of bed, and plaited a great big blanket of straw, and carried it off, and spread it over the dead bird, and piled upon it thistle-down as soft as cotton wool, which he had found in the field mouse's room, so that the poor little thing should lie warmly buried.

"Farewell, pretty little bird!" he said. "Farewell, and thank you for your beautiful songs in the summer, when the trees were green, and the sun shone down warmly on us!" Then he laid his head against the bird's heart. But the bird was not dead: she had been frozen, but now that he had warmed her, she was coming to life again.

In autumn, the swallows fly away to foreign lands; but there are some who are late in starting, and then they get so cold that they drop down as if dead, and the snow comes and covers them over.

Thumbelin trembled, he was so frightened; for the bird was very large in comparison with himself – only an inch high. But he took courage, piled up the down more closely over the poor swallow, fetched his own coverlid and laid it over her head.

Next night he crept out again to her. There she was alive, but very weak; she could only open her eyes for a moment and look at Thumbelin, who was standing in front of her with a piece of rotten wood in his hand, for he had no other lantern.

"Thank you, pretty little child!" said the swallow to him. "'I am so beautifully warm! Soon I shall regain my strength, and then I shall be able to fly out again into the warm sunshine."

"Oh!" he said, "it is very cold outside; it is snowing and freezing! Stay in your warm bed; I will take care of you!"

Then he brought her water in a petal, which she drank, after which she related to him how she had torn one of her wings on a bramble, so that she could not fly as fast as the other swallows, who had flown far away to warmer lands. So at last she had dropped down exhausted, and then she could remember no more. The whole winter she remained down there, and Thumbelin looked after her and nursed her tenderly. Neither the mole nor the field mouse learnt anything of this, for they could not bear the poor swallow.

When the spring came, and the sun warmed the earth again, the swallow said farewell to Thumbelin, who opened the hole in the roof for her which the mole had made. The sun shone brightly down upon him, and the swallow asked him if he would go with her; he could sit upon her back. Thumbelin wanted very much to fly far away into the green wood, but he knew that the old field mouse would be sad if he ran away. "No, I mustn't come!" he said.

"Farewell, dear good little boy!" said the swallow, and flew off into the sunshine. Thumbelin gazed after her with the tears standing in his eyes, for he was very fond of the swallow.

"Tweet, tweet!" sang the bird, and flew into the green wood. Thumbelin was very unhappy. He was not allowed to go out

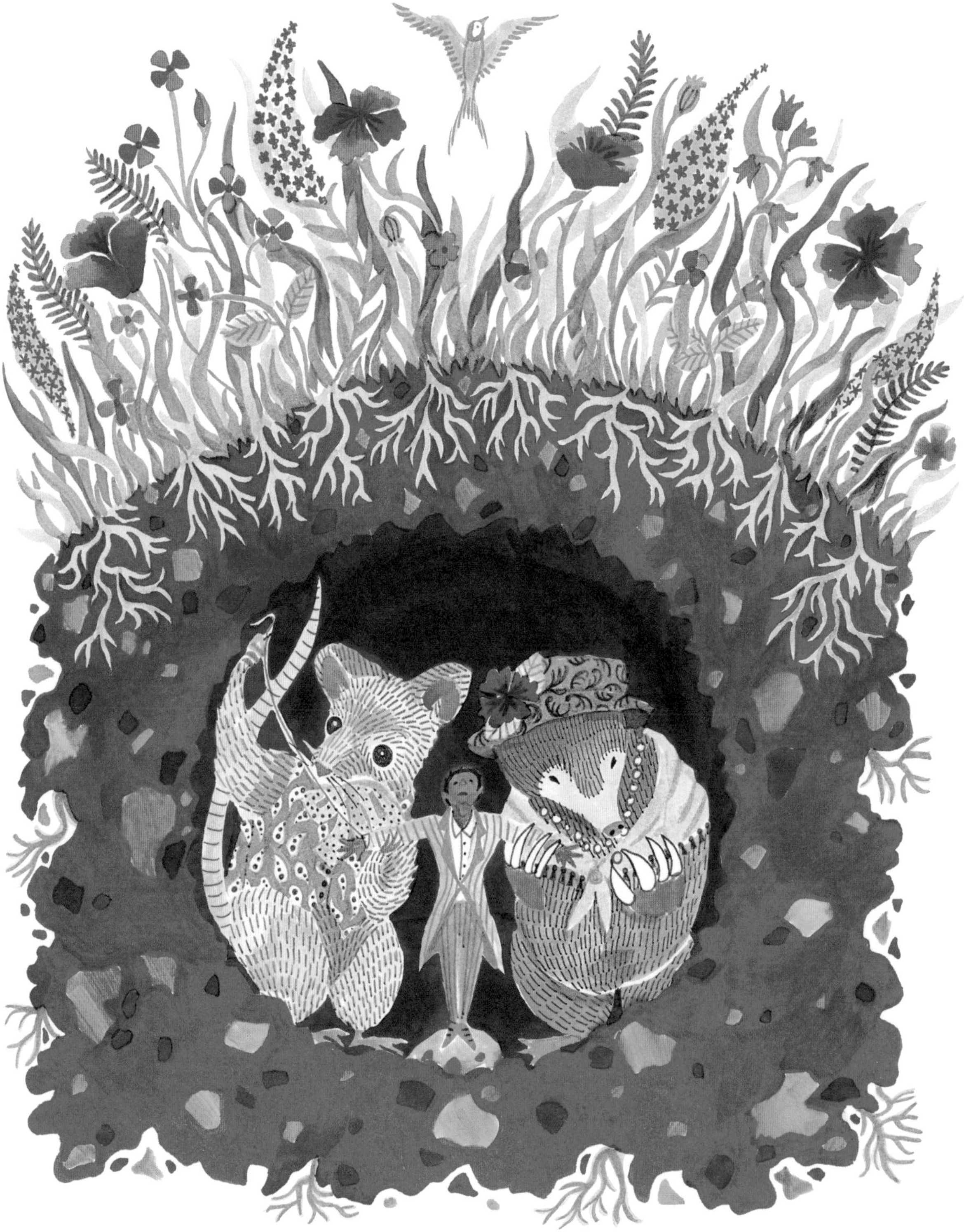

into the warm sunshine. The corn which had been sowed in the field over the field mouse's home grew up high into the air, and made a thick forest for the poor little boy, who was only an inch high.

"Now you are to be a groom, Thumbelin!" said the field mouse, "for our neighbour has proposed for you! What a piece of fortune for a poor child like you! Now you must set to work at your linen for your dowry, for nothing must be lacking if you are to become the husband of our neighbour, the mole!"

Thumbelin had to spin all day long, and every evening the mole visited him, and told him that when the summer was over the sun would not shine so hot; now it was burning the earth as hard as a stone. Yes, when the summer had passed, they would keep the wedding.

But he was not at all pleased about it, for he did not like the stupid mole. Every morning when the sun was rising, and every evening when it was setting, he would steal out of the house-door, and when the breeze parted the ears of corn so that he could see the blue sky through them, he thought how bright and beautiful it must be outside, and longed to see his dear swallow again. But she never came; no doubt she had flown away far into the great green wood.

By the autumn Thumbelin had finished the dowry.

"In four weeks you will be married!" said the field mouse; "don't be obstinate, or I shall bite you with my sharp white teeth! You will get a fine wife! The Queen herself has not such a velvet coat. Her storeroom and cellar are full, and you should be thankful for that."

Well, the wedding day arrived. The mole had come to fetch Thumbelin to live with her deep down under the ground, never to come out into the warm sun again, for that was what she didn't like. The poor little boy was very sad; for now he must say goodbye to the beautiful sun.

"Farewell, bright sun!" he cried, stretching out his arms towards it, and taking another step outside the house; for now the corn had been reaped, and only the dry stubble was left standing. "Farewell, farewell!" he said, and put his arms round a little red flower that grew there. "Give my love to the dear swallow when you see her!"

"Tweet, tweet!" sounded in his ear all at once. He looked up. There was the swallow flying past! As soon as she saw Thumbelin, she was very glad. He told her how unwilling he was to marry the ugly mole, as then he had to live underground where the sun never shone, and he could not help bursting into tears.

"The cold winter is coming now," said the swallow. "I must fly away to warmer lands: will you come with me? You can sit on my back, and we will fly far away from the ugly mole and her dark house, over the mountains, to the warm countries where the sun shines more brightly than here, where it is always summer, and there are always beautiful flowers. Do come with me, dear little Thumbelin, who saved my life when I lay frozen in the dark tunnel!"

"Yes, I will go with you," said Thumbelin, and got on the swallow's back, with his feet on one of her outstretched wings. Up she flew into the air, over woods and seas, over the great mountains where the snow is always lying. And if he was cold he crept under her warm feathers, only keeping his little head out to admire all the beautiful things in the world beneath. At last they came to warm lands; there the sun was brighter, the sky seemed twice as high, and in the hedges hung the finest green and purple grapes; in the woods grew oranges and lemons: the air was scented with myrtle and mint, and on the roads were pretty little children running about and playing with great gorgeous butterflies. But the swallow flew on farther, and it became more and more beautiful. Under the most splendid green trees beside a blue lake stood a glittering white-marble castle. Vines hung about the high pillars; there were many swallows' nests, and in one of these lived the swallow who was carrying Thumbelin.

"Here is my house!" said she. "But it won't do for you to live with me; I am not tidy enough to please you. Find a home for yourself in one of the lovely flowers that grow down there; now I will set you down, and you can do whatever you like."

"That will be splendid!" said he, clapping his little hands.

There lay a great white marble column which had fallen to the ground and broken into three pieces, but between these grew the most beautiful white flowers. The swallow flew down with Thumbelin, and set him upon one of the broad leaves. But there, to his astonishment, he found a tiny little woman sitting in the middle of the flower, as white and transparent as if she were made of glass; she had the prettiest golden crown on her head, and the most beautiful wings on her shoulders; she herself was no bigger than Thumbelin. She was the spirit of the flower. In each blossom there dwelt a tiny woman or man; but this one was the Queen over the others.

"How handsome she is!" whispered Thumbelin to the swallow.

The little Princess was very much frightened at the swallow, for in comparison with one so tiny as herself she seemed a giantess. But when she saw Thumbelin, she was delighted, for he was the most beautiful boy she had ever seen. So she took her golden crown from off her head and put it on his, asking him his name, and if he would be her husband, and then he would be King of all the flowers. Yes! she was a different kind of wife to the daughter of the toad and the mole with the black-velvet coat. So he said "Yes" to the noble Princess. And out of each flower came a gentleman and lady, each so tiny and pretty that it was a pleasure to see them. Each brought Thumbelin a present, but the best of all was a beautiful pair of wings which were fastened on to his back, and now he too could fly from flower to flower. They all wished him joy, and the swallow sat above in her nest and sang the wedding march, and that she did as well as she could; but she was sad, because she was very fond of Thumbelin and did not want to be separated from him.

"You shall not be called Thumbelin!" said the spirit of the flower to him; "that is an ugly name, and you are much too pretty for that. We will call you Mr Blossom."

"Farewell, farewell!" said the little swallow with a heavy heart, and flew away to farther lands, far, far away, right back to Denmark. There she had a little nest above a window, where her husband lived, who can tell fairy stories. "Tweet, tweet!" she sang to him. And that is the way we learnt the whole story.

ACKNOWLEDGEMENTS

A massive thank you to all the fairy godmothers and fairy god-fathers who magicked this book into existence. To Andrew and Leonora Blanche Lang, the other wife-and-husband team, who were behind *The Blue Fairy Book* (1889), *The Red Fairy Book* (1890) and *The Yellow Fairy Book* (1894) whose public domain texts we've used. The Langs edited and translated fairy tales, including those collected and written by Charles Perrault ('Little Red Riding Hood', 'Cinderella', 'Sleeping Beauty' and 'Puss in Boots'), Gabrielle-Suzanne de Villeneuve ('Beauty and the Beast'), Jacob Ludwig Karl Grimm and Wilhelm Carl Grimm ('Hansel and Gretel', 'Rumpelstiltskin', 'Snowdrop', 'Rapunzel') and Hans Christian Andersen ('Thumbelina').

To our agent Sophie Lambert for her support, diplomacy and her magic-making on a busy train to Edinburgh. To our editor Louisa Joyner for the passion, energy and ideas that she brought to every aspect of this book (including the gender of chickens). To Donna Payne for her brilliant eyes, thoughtful feedback and disturbing movie recommendations. To our team at Faber & Faber for their hard work including Jack

Murphy, Libby Marshall, Claire Cross, Kate Ward and everyone at Altaimage. And also to the rest of the Faber team: Leah Thaxton, Sarah Lough, Sophie Portas, Bethany Carter, Hannah Styles, Lizzie Bishop, Hattie Cooke, Emma Cheshire, Rachel Darling and Catherine Daly, for all their hard work. To Katie Greenstreet, Louise Emslie-Smith and Meredith Ford at C+W Agency for their help and patience with our countless annoying emails. To Sarah Burton and Bryony Hall at the Society of Authors for their advice. To the British Library for helping us access the beautiful original texts.

A huge, heartfelt thank you to Alexa von Hirschberg, who gave Karrie coffee and courage to turn our idea into a reality. To Jonny Fransman for his eagle eyes and wolf heart. To our family for keeping us supported and to uncle Sam Ludwin who we dearly miss. To all our smallest lovies who we hope will read this tucked up in bed – Isla, Rafi, Evie, Caspar, Thomas, James, Max and Orla. To Den Pen, always, for her infectious enthusiasm. To Mike Medaglia and Miriam Robinson for their early advice. To the Ibiza gang – Hannah Berry, Simone Lia and Nicola Streeten for making this job a little less lonely and that bat ring a little harder to win. To our parents for all those bedtime stories that made us imagine a world that could be different to our own. And most of all to our daughter, Lyra, who we hope will continue to feel free to be a dragon, queen or big, bad wolf, whenever she pleases.